THE RISE AND FALL OF

DEREK COWELL

THE RISE AND FALL OF
DEREK COWELL

VALERIE SHERRARD

The publisher gratefully acknowledges the support of the Canada Council
for the Arts and the Ontario Arts Council for its publishing program.
We acknowledge the financial support of the Government of Canada through
the Canada Book Fund (CBF) for our publishing activities, and the Government of
Ontario through Ontario Creates, an agency of the Ontario Ministry of Culture,
and the Ontario Book Publishing Tax Credit Program.

LIBRARY AND ARCHIVES CANADA CATALOGUING IN PUBLICATION

Title: The rise and fall of Derek Cowell / by Valerie Sherrard.
Names: Sherrard, Valerie, author.
Identifiers: Canadiana (print) 20190230762 | Canadiana (ebook) 20190230754 |
ISBN 9781770865747 (softcover) | ISBN 9781770865754 (HTML)
Classification: LCC PS8587.H3867 R57 2020 | DDC jc813/.54—dc23

United States Library of Congress Control Number: 2019955756
Cover illustration and design: David Jardine
Interior text design: Tannice Goddard, tannicegdesigns.ca

Printed and bound in Canada.
Manufactured by Friesens in Altona, Manitoba, Canada
in September 2020.

DCB
AN IMPRINT OF CORMORANT BOOKS INC.
260 SPADINA AVENUE, SUITE 502, TORONTO, ONTARIO, M5T 2E4
www.dcbyoungreaders.com
www.cormorantbooks.com

For my granddaughter Veronicka.
Let truth guide your way.

CHAPTER ONE

Nothing ever happens in a small town.

No, that's not quite true. What I *should* have said is nothing *new* ever happens in a small town. Repetition is the relentless norm, and that leaves you completely unprepared for change, if it ever comes.

Here in Breval (population 4,300 according to the sign) life was so boring that some of my more memorable moments were actually *non*-happenings. Like last summer, when the family headed out on vacation and left me behind.

Yes, you heard me right.

And sure, they only got a couple of blocks before my parents realized I wasn't in the van. They came back, but that's not the point. My sisters were all there, buckled in safe and sound. You'd think the fact that the family's only *male* offspring was missing would have stood out, but *that* somehow escaped everyone's attention. (Mom gave me a weird excuse about the picnic cooler being in my spot. Because, who doesn't mistake a big hunk of orange plastic for one of their kids every now and then?)

In an effort to salvage a scrap of dignity, I developed a theory. I decided I possessed secret powers of invisibility.

Under different circumstances, I'd have been all for that. Cool, superhero invisibility, for example, would have been excellent. Zipping around, performing sneaky feats to put villains in their place, and maybe doing a little eavesdropping.

But *my* brand of transparency was nothing like that. It was as if people actually did not see me, as though I somehow failed to register in the realm of human detection.

Sounds like an exaggeration, I know, but I could tell you a dozen stories to back it up. Like the day in science lab when a classmate asked if I knew whether or not Derek Cowell was there yet.

I'm Derek Cowell.

Or the time we were on a field trip and I had to make a quick dash to the bathroom just before the bus was leaving to go back to the school. Theoretically, there was no danger it would leave without me — we had a buddy system *and* a checklist.

Except somehow, my name got missed when they were going down the list, and my "buddy" never said a word.

Asked about it later, he said he plain forgot who his buddy was. No one else forgot their buddies that day and if it hadn't been for a delay at the stop sign on the corner, I might still be there, staring forlornly at the spot the bus used to be. As it was, I barely got to it and pounded on the door before it pulled away.

See what I mean? I'm Derek, the see-through teen.

For the most part I didn't mind being overlooked. Now and then, usually when I did something moronic, it could even be a plus. Either way, I was used to it. After all, it's been this way for as long as I can remember. (Or I should say, it *was* that way until a freak occurrence changed everything. I'll get to that in a minute.) At home, a big factor was the amount of attention that's left to dribble down when a guy lives in a house full of girls.

I have three sisters. If that doesn't horrify you then you don't have three sisters. Or you're a girl yourself, and your only reason for reading this story is that you heard about the embarrassing parts.

Living with three sisters means I spend a lot of time listening to girl talk. Not that I don't try to protect myself, but I can hardly ever find my earbuds when I need them. That's because *one of my sisters* has "borrowed" them, which is known as stealing in parts of the civilized world that do not include the house I live in.

Kim is the oldest at fifteen, which also means she's incredibly sophisticated — in her imagination. Kim and her friends have made an art of sighing, rolling their eyes, and raising their eyebrows at each other. It's as if they belong to a secret society that's only allowed to communicate through facial expressions.

Other than that, their favorite pastime seems to be holding thoughtful discussions on important world events. I'm kidding, of course. They mostly talk about romance, but they work in a few other things like clothes and hair products too. Probably so they won't seem shallow.

Steffie Morton is the only one of Kim's friends who *isn't* like that. She's friendly and funny and not one bit hard to look at. Of all the people who hang out at our house, she's the one I'd most like some attention from. Which was a big part of how this all started — but that's getting ahead of things. I was telling you about my sisters.

Next in line is Paige, who lives and breathes drama. We're both thirteen at the moment, but I'm older by ten months. There is nothing that can't be turned into a matter of life and death if Paige is in the room. As a result, her vocabulary has shrunk to the point that it includes a mere four adjectives. They are: worst, best and WORST,

BEST. (Okay, that's actually only two, at different deci-bels, but I didn't want her to sound like a dunce.)

Paige claims to have a boyfriend. Mom says that is *not happening* at her age. According to Paige that makes her the WORST mother ever. The guy goes by Junior, but I never know if that's a real name or not. He's about as interesting as a blank page, so unless my sister is attracted to dull, I'd say she's trying to get Mom going. Some form of weird female rebellion, maybe.

Either way, it's not my problem except for the odd time when Mom and Dad are out and she sneaks Junior in. Then I feel obligated to give him menacing looks — you know, to make sure he knows I'm around. Watching. Not that there's been anything to see. Paige hasn't even tried the standard "We're going to my room to listen to music" bit. And when they're sitting in the living room he's usually alone on the couch while she flops in her favorite chair. It's obvious she has zero actual interest in the guy. I think of him as a sort of stuffed toy she's bored with but drags around anyway because she likes the attention it gets her.

Anna is the youngest, at nine. She's also the family extortionist. And let me just say, if you've never been blackmailed, chances are pretty good you're an only child.

She's little and cute and looks so innocent when she's standing there with her hand out, leveling those cold eyes at you, it makes the chill traveling down your spine seem a bit surreal. But that kid is merciless.

Pleading with Anna gets you nowhere. You can tell her any sob story you like, it won't do you a bit of good. Once you're cornered, you're as good as finished. I've learned not to bother wasting my breath. I just fork over the cash and watch her pocket it on her way out the door.

I always know exactly where she's going with her ill-gotten gains. Anna is like some kind of animal shelter Robin Hood. Every cent she gets her hands on goes to help feed the cats and dogs and whatever else they house in that place. (Half of them would probably have starved to death long ago if it wasn't for me.)

Not that she's all bad. Anna fluctuates from being the worst of the lot to the only one with any redeeming qualities. She reminds me of a poem Mom used to recite — about a little girl who was either very, very good, or horrid.

Given that she lives to blackmail, I'm positive Anna would pick horrid. The good thing (if there can be anything good about being shaken down) is that Anna is too young to ask for much. She also never tries to double dip and she keeps her mouth shut once you've bought her silence.

Fortunately, there's another, non-criminal side to Anna. That side would save you the last cookie even if she wanted it herself, or cover you with a blanket if you fell asleep on the couch. She's a living, breathing contradiction, my youngest sister. The same girl who can take your last dollar with a heart of frozen stone will also sob her head off over a bird with a broken wing.

You'll get to know more about all of us soon, but first, I need to go back to a day in April and the moment small-town life went from boring to bizarre.

CHAPTER TWO

Steve was at my place. (If Paige was telling this story, she'd describe Steve as my BFF and fabricate a heartwarming story about how we met, preferably one that included rescuing a kitten. Since I'm not Paige, I'll just call him Steve and get on with it.)

We weren't doing anything much — hanging out, talking about ways we could earn some extra cash, that kind of thing. Eventually, we got around to raiding the kitchen. Mom gets on health kicks now and then, but fortunately this wasn't one of those nightmarish times. We found a bag of some sort of cheesy puffs and filled a bowl.

Our munch-fest was interrupted by the sound of the front door opening, followed by a burst of giggles and excited chatter. (I've learned this is some sort of mandatory thing Kim's friends do when they come into the house, although it's never actually related to anything funny or exciting.)

A moment later we heard the bunch of them heading down the hall toward the kitchen. Steve raised an eyebrow, reached into the snack bowl and grabbed as many puffs as he could hold. Just in time too. In seconds, the kitchen was full of girls and a minute after that the cheese puff bowl held nothing but a sprinkling of orange dust.

Being in the same room as Kim's friends had a strange effect on Steve. For starters, he stopped slouching. That can be a sign of embarrassing things to come. I tried not to look.

Turns out that wasn't too hard, since Steffie chose that moment to smile at me and say, "Hey, Derek. What's up?"

That was new. Not that Steffie had never spoken to me before — she usually says, "Hi," or gives me a friendly wave or something. But an actual question; I was not prepared for *that*.

A string of babble lurched out of my mouth. As it echoed in my brain, it sounded something like, "Whar fretsal stuck merkin blurry smick smick plum."

There *were* a few actual words in there somewhere, but it's anyone's guess what they might have meant.

To her credit, Steffie didn't break and run. She stood there, with her smile a little frozen, nodding like she was encouraging a small child to perform some simple task.

That was when I noticed a girl I'd never seen before. She had short, dirty-blonde hair that hung around her eyes in wild wisps. I'd have said she was cute, except she was smirking rudely. At me.

She'd been standing slightly behind Steffie, but she moved forward to get a better look at the gibberish-spewing clown.

"That was quite a sentence," she said.

Her comment got Steve's attention. "It's a secret language," he said, smoothly.

"*Top* secret," I agreed. Except, Steve was busy introducing himself and getting her name, which was Riley, and I don't think either one of them heard me.

I switched my attention back to Steffie, but all we did was exchange awkward smiles. It was a relief when the girls decided to move along to some other part of the house.

"Okay, well, see you later," Steffie said.

"You're welcome," I answered. (A bit of brilliance that played itself over and over in my head when I was trying to fall asleep that night.)

Steve didn't mention the gaffe, although he had to have heard it. He knows I have a thing for Steffie — not that I've ever said so. We prefer to let things like that hang in the air, unsaid. It's the way of testosterone.

He leaned forward once the girls had cleared out.

"I'm pretty sure Riley is into me," he said. Unlike me, Steve doesn't struggle with confidence issues.

"And I'm pretty sure you're losing your grip on reality."

"Yeah? Well, I'll tell you what I *didn't* lose my grip on," he said, lifting his left hand from under the table. He was still holding the fistful of cheesy puffs, although I can't say there was much puff left in them. Crushed or maybe melted, they looked disgusting. Steve shoved some into his mouth, chewed a bit and smiled. Not an appetizing sight.

"Too bad Riley can't see you now," I said.

Steve laughed. He finished the rest and went to the sink to wash his hands. The orange smudges he left on the towel suggested he hadn't killed himself scrubbing. I grabbed the towel and took it down the hall to the laundry room hamper so Mom wouldn't see it.

Upstairs, I could hear voices raised over the music. I paused to listen for a few seconds, but it was all garbled.

"She'll probably be asking around about me," Steve said as soon as I walked back into the kitchen.

"Who?"

"What do you mean, who? Who were we talking about?"

"Right, sorry. Riley. So what, exactly, did you think she was going to be asking?"

"You know, whether I'm available or whatever. She might even ask you."

"Yeah, that happens a lot. I'm getting sick of Kim's friends asking about you."

He laughed. "They can't help themselves."

"Some of them have managed to," I said.

"The sad thing is, there's only one of me to go around," Steve said.

"A terrible loss for females everywhere."

"That's true. But I noticed Steffie made a point of talking to *you*," he said, suddenly serious.

"She always says 'hello' or something. She's just being polite."

"If you say so."

I can't say I minded when a text alert cut that conversation off. Steve stood and dug his phone out of his pocket. He frowned as he read the message.

"Oops," he said. "I gotta go. I forgot Mom's latest prospect is coming for supper."

"So why do you have to go home *now*?"

"To clean my room. Mom doesn't want the guy to know she's raising a slob. Might scare him off."

"And yet, she's letting him meet you. Strange."

"What's strange is the idea that this guy would even *see* my room," Steve said. "I pointed that out, but then Mom told me some weird story about having to move the couch in front of company once. Half the time I don't have a clue what she's talking about."

"Yeah, it's the same with my mom."

I went with him to the door and stood there as he turned down the sidewalk toward his house. He might have more luck with girls than I do, but I wouldn't trade places with him when it comes to family life. Even three annoying sisters weren't so bad when I thought of how weird it would be if my mom was out there — dating. Gross.

Steve seems to take it all in stride.

I stepped back into the house and started up the stairs to my room. Giggles to my right drew my attention to the living room archway where the girls had now congregated. Steffie, Kim and a couple of others were just inside the arch, arms slung across each other's backs. It looked like they were going to do some type of group thing — a cheer or dance or something.

I paused on the fifth step and leaned forward. The way Steffie was smiling made my heart do something weird. It wasn't until I heard Riley's phone click that I realized they'd been standing there posing for a group selfie.

I moved on feeling a bit cheated. But that was only because I had no idea what had just happened.

If I'd known that, I would have been terrified.

CHAPTER THREE

For the record, I don't usually look like a demented Disney character.

It was Crystal Rutherford, a girl in my history class, who first texted me the picture. Within a few minutes, it arrived via three other people and after that it turned into a flood. Sometimes there was a message, or a caption, or even an emoticon or two with it, but the image never altered.

There I was, Derek Alexander Cowell, hanging over the stair railing, gawking idiotically at the group of girls below. Their innocent smiles drew a sharp contrast to the slightly deranged face hovering above their heads.

When the first shock wore off, a numb sort of dread descended on me. Just the thought of the reactions I'd have to face made me queasy. Anybody could see I was ogling one of the girls — heck, I was practically drooling. The only thing that wasn't obvious was *which* lucky girl was the target of my yearning gaze.

I could only hope that meant Steffie hadn't felt the need to get a restraining order. Yet.

Not once did it occur to me that anything good could come of this. Which made the reception I got at school the next morning quite a surprise. I used a back entrance and tried to slink unseen to my locker, but I was spotted going through the science department.

"Derek, you dog!"

I lifted my head to see who'd called my name. Kamau Rop. We have a couple of classes together and we've shot hoops a few times. He's a good guy, so I hoped he'd go easy on me. I pasted a weak smile on my face, to show what a good sport I was.

"Nice work!" He was grinning widely. "Those girls had no idea whatsoever."

I blinked. I also kept my mouth shut, since opening it could only have given away my confusion.

By the time I'd been congratulated by four or five people, I'd clued in to what was happening. Everyone thought I'd done it on purpose. And in that light, my expression in the photo had taken on a completely different meaning. Instead of being a guy panting over someone he knows is out of his league, I was a performer, a jester, a stairway lurker, getting one over on my chosen prey.

In an instant, I'd been transformed into a middle school photobomb celebrity. I was fist-bumped, high-fived and slapped on the shoulder. People who'd never spoken to me before came over to yuk it up.

It was the first time in my history as a student at Breval Middle School that I wished the day would last longer. It flew by.

It hadn't occurred to me that the reaction to the picture would continue on outside of school and into my house. Actually, I'd assumed my sisters would make rude comments which I'd ignore and that would be the end of it. Wrong.

Mom and Dad got home from work about the same time, like they do most days. Dad came in carrying a big bag of takeout from Have Happy, a local restaurant that offers a variety of Asian cuisine. The smell of the food trailed after him, making my mouth water as he headed toward the back of the house.

Paige picked up the scent and dashed to the dining room to set the table. Within minutes we were all seated, poking into the cardboard boxes, scooping out our favorites from the assortment of foods. It was a nice mix, and I was concentrating on filling my plate when Kim spoke.

"I hate to have to tell you what kind of son you're

raising," she said, pausing for effect. "But Derek photo-bombed a picture of me and my friends yesterday."

Dad paused in the middle of spooning Pad Thai onto his plate. He frowned at me while Mom said, "What? Derek! You were raised better than that."

"Do you even know what a photobomb is?" I asked.

"Well, it doesn't sound very nice, whatever it is."

"He *ruined* the picture," Kim said.

"It's sooo funny though," Paige said. "It looks like he's crushing their heads."

I looked across the table at her. Was there a second picture out there, somewhere? Or had I missed something?

I slid my phone out of my pocket and swiped it to life under the table. There's a dumb rule at our house about no phones at mealtime, but if you're smooth you can get away with it.

"Derek's texting or something," Kim said. I made a mental note to make sure she gets caught the next time she sneaks out after curfew.

"Derek?" Dad gave me a stern look. He held his hand out and I passed my phone over.

"I was just going to show you the picture, so you could see it's no big deal," I claimed.

Dad passed the phone back saying, "I'd like to see it."

I tapped the picture up on the screen and took a quick

look before I surrendered it again. Paige was right — I don't know how I hadn't noticed it before. Too focused on my goofy face, I guess.

My hands were positioned on the stair railing in a way that looked *exactly* like the girls' heads were being squeezed between them.

Dad stared at the picture for a few seconds, shook his head the way he does when he can't figure out why his kids are so strange, and handed it off to Mom.

Mom took longer looking the picture over. Her eyebrows went up and she sighed a couple of times, but that was it. I could tell neither of my folks was going to take Kim's side, no matter how upset she pretended to be.

I was in the clear.

And then Anna, who was the only one at the table who hadn't yet seen it, asked if she could have a look. Mom gave her the phone and she spent a full minute or more studying the shot. A couple of times she enlarged parts of it.

When she was finished, she leaned toward me.

"Here you go, Derek," she said sweetly.

I reached across the table, met her eyes and felt my heart sink.

The family blackmailer knew.

CHAPTER FOUR

I couldn't help wondering: why? Of all the people who'd seen the picture, why did *Anna* have to be the one who suspected there was more to it than an innocent photobomb?

Okay, so, technically, Anna wasn't the *only* person who read my expression correctly and knew I was looking mushy-faced-love-struck at one of the girls below. Steve got it the second he saw it. But Steve wasn't about to blackmail me. If I knew my sister, this was going to be her biggest score ever. I spent some time trying to figure out what she'd ask for so I could be ready with some negotiating strategies, but she didn't give any hints. Not right away.

Anna wasn't dumb. Chances were good she'd think it over, weigh her options and hit me with her demands when my defenses were at their lowest. Or on allowance day.

But … if the right kind of distraction came along, she *could* forget all about the picture. My hopes for that happening skyrocketed the next morning when word got out that Luna Amatulli had been spotted in town.

Yes. *The* Luna Amatulli, teen star of the wildly popular TV series, *Palomino Gal.*

Luna comes to Breval for the weekend every now and then. She visits her grandparents and always keeps a seriously low profile. If she *is* spotted, the entire teenage population turns into a selfie-crazed mob.

Okay, maybe not a mob. We don't have enough teenagers to form a crowd that size. But there are quite a few of them out there skulking around, hoping to get a picture with Luna. Not with her and *them* — she makes it clear she's not here to mingle. A selfie with Luna in the background is enough to be considered a score. Like I said, there's not a lot going on in Breval.

As for me, I'd rather be doing *nothing* than peeking around corners looking for some actress who wants to be left alone. I told that to Steve when he showed up at my place late Saturday morning, put on an innocent face and casually suggested we go for a walk.

"Man, what is wrong with you?" he grumbled. "Have you seen how gorgeous this girl is?"

"There are lots of gorgeous girls on the planet," I pointed out.

"Yeah, but this one is right here, right now!" he said.

"Don't care," I said. He shrugged.

"Okay, so I'll go myself," he said.

"See ya," I told him and answered his shrug with one of my own.

That's when my mom came into the kitchen with Anna in tow.

"Derek, I need you to take your sister to the drugstore."

"Do I have to go now?" I said. "Steve just got here."

Even as the words came out of my mouth I could practically feel Steve's hands on my back, getting ready to shove me under the bus.

"That's okay, Derek," he said cheerfully. "I'll come with you guys."

The next thing I knew we were on our way to buy Bristol board for Anna. It wasn't even for school either, just one of her lamebrain club ideas for kids who love cats or something. I wasn't really listening as she explained it.

We'd made the purchase and were about to leave when Anna let out a screech.

"Oh, NO!"

My razor-sharp reflexes made me take a stumbling jump backward, which knocked Steve into a stand of used books. He flailed and managed to catch it before it went crashing to the floor, but a bunch of paperbacks flew out. They landed on and around a customer we hadn't noticed, since she was crouched down in the next aisle.

It was Luna Amatulli!

She came storming out of hiding with her eyes blazing.

"What's wrong, little girl?" she asked Anna. "What did these awful boys do?"

Anna blinked. She looked and me and Steve and then back at Luna.

"Nothing," she said.

"Then why did you scream 'Oh, NO!'" Luna pressed.

"I forgot to get a black marker," Anna said. "I'm making a poster."

"And we're *not* awful," Steve said.

Luna ignored that. Her attention had moved to a pair of girls approaching the door. They hadn't yet spotted Luna, whose face was transformed with panic.

"Please!" she implored us. "Hide me!"

We did. We formed a combination human/Bristol board shield while Anna launched into an insanely boring description of her plans for the poster.

Fortunately, the girls found what they came in for, paid and left in a matter of minutes. If they noticed our odd group, oddly posed, they deliberately ignored us.

Luna stood upright again once the coast was clear.

"Thanks," she said. "Sorry I called you awful."

"You're probably thinking we're more like heroes now, huh?" Steve said, grinning.

But Luna had turned toward the cash register, manned by Mr. Holst, the store owner. "I'm going to go," she said.

Mr. Holst nodded. "You tell your grandpa I'll be over to beat him at a game of checkers one of these days."

Luna gave him a smile and hurried to the back of the store and into a room marked "Employees Only."

"She uses the back door!" Steve said. "So no one sees her on the street."

"Don't order a deerstalker cap just yet, Sherlock," said Mr. Holst. Then he told Anna, "The markers are at the back of aisle three, Miss."

Anna got what she needed and we left. As we neared my house Steve finally stopped repeating things like, "Can you believe it!" and "We actually talked to her!"

He stopped because his brain had moved on to the tragic part of our encounter.

"And we never even got a picture!" he lamented. "No one's going to believe we met Luna Amatulli without proof."

"*I* have proof," Anna claimed calmly.

Steve and I swung around to face her.

"What do you mean, you have proof?" he asked.

She held up her iPod.

"I took a picture," she said.

CHAPTER FIVE

We stared at the photo on Anna's device for a long couple of minutes. Steve was the first to speak.

"Huh," he said.

"How'd you take a picture without her noticing?" I asked Anna.

"She was talking to Mr. Holst," Anna said. She peered down at the photo and added, "Hey! It sort of looks like she's going to kiss Derek on the cheek."

Even I hadn't missed that. It *one hundred percent* looked like she was about to kiss me. Her face was close to mine and her lips were puckered from whatever she'd been saying to Mr. Holst.

Unfortunately for Steve, he was on the other side of Luna, so she was turned away from him.

"You probably shouldn't show that around," Steve said. "I think we should respect her privacy, especially now that we actually met her."

"I thought you wanted proof you talked to her," Anna said.

"I wasn't thinking straight," he answered. "But, yeah. *This* is the right thing to do. Don't you think so, Derek?"

"Sure," I said.

"Okay," Anna agreed.

Steve looked pleased at how easy it had been to persuade us. I, on the other hand, knew it didn't matter. I could have told him what was going to happen next, but I figured he'd find out soon enough.

It was even sooner than I'd have predicted.

As she'd promised, Anna didn't show the picture around. She *only* shared it with Paige and Kim, who immediately texted it to everyone they knew.

My phone started pinging first, but it was only seconds later that Steve's lit up too. We'd been back at my place for nine minutes.

It took a lot longer — an entire week in fact — before he stopped being grumpy about it. In fairness, I know Steve didn't actually begrudge me the boost in popularity. What he minded was how the normal order of things had reversed. Suddenly, I was the one everyone noticed, and *he* was the invisible friend.

He finally brought it up one day when we were at his

place, a female-free sanctuary. Well, technically his mom is a female, but I'm not counting mothers.

Steve had gone into the kitchen to grab us each a can of Pepsi while I kicked back on the couch. His return sent his dog Slipper into a fit of barking and jumping and hanging his tongue halfway to the floor, as if he hadn't just seen him two minutes ago. Steve waited for that bit of insanity to settle down before he started talking.

"I've been thinking about this whole situation," he said. "Specifically, ways we can maximize the benefits."

"What benefits?" I asked.

He shook his head. "Seriously? How many girls have come up and talked to you since this started?"

A smile spread itself across my face. "A lot."

"And before that, how many girls talked to you on an average day?"

"I dunno. Not that many."

Or, more accurately, zero, unless you counted comments like, "Oww! Watch it!" or "Look where you're going, klutz!" when I accidentally stepped on someone's foot.

"Exactly!" Steve said.

"Except, these things never last," I pointed out.

"*Unless* —"Steve paused, spreading his hands slowly in front of him. "Unless you *make* it last."

"How do I do that?" I asked, getting interested.

Steve shook his head and rolled his eyes.

"*You* are *completely* hopeless," he said.

"I got that from the head shaking and eye rolling," I told him.

"It's a wonder."

I let that go. "So, what are you thinking?"

"There's got to be a way to keep this thing going."

"I dunno," I said. "Flukes like that don't happen every day."

"So we figure out how to *make* it happen," Steve said. "With something we can both be in on."

"Yeah, that would be good," I agreed. It was the closest Steve had come to admitting he was feeling left out.

I gulped down some Pepsi, belched and said, "Would a video work? I saw a really cool one the other day of a guy doing amazing skateboarding tricks. What about something like that?"

The look Steve gave me told me how unimpressed he was, even before he spoke.

"That's perfect, except for one thing. Neither one of us skateboards. We'd probably kill ourselves."

"Right. I guess we'd have to practice a lot for something like that."

"And since when are girls interested in skateboarding stunts?" Steve said. "We've got to think of something funny, or the kind of cute thing a lot of girls get excited over."

"My sisters go crazy over animals," I said. "Videos, pictures — whatever. They're nuts about that stuff. Especially cats."

"I think you're onto something," Steve said. "Maybe some pictures of kittens with funny captions. And us in the background like we're hiding or sneaking up or whatever."

The only problem was, neither one of us had a cat. I pointed that out to Steve.

"The animal shelter does, though," Steve said. "They're always looking for people to take cats — the place is overrun with them!"

I liked that idea. And after years of being blackmailed into helping feed the shelter animals, it was about time the place gave something back to me.

"So, could we borrow some kittens for a couple of days?" I asked.

"Doubt it. They don't even let people adopt them without filling in a bunch of forms. That's how we got Slipper."

I vaguely remembered them getting Slipper, but hadn't known he'd been a rescue. It was right at the time that Steve's folks split up. His mom decided they should have a guard dog; she said she felt vulnerable now that she was a single parent.

Not a lot of people who wanted a guard dog would have picked Slipper. I don't know what kind of dog he is — I doubt anyone does — but he barely comes up to my knees, can't weigh more than twenty-five pounds, and is about the friendliest animal I've ever seen. Unless the plan was to have him lick an intruder to death, Slipper wasn't going to be much protection to anyone.

None of that mattered now. We needed kittens, and from what Steve had just said, the shelter wasn't going to be much help.

But that was only because he hadn't told me the rest of his idea.

"We can *volunteer*!" he explained, grinning.

"What? At the shelter?"

"Exactly. That will give us access to all kinds of kittens. We'll have our pick of the lot for our video."

It sounded like a reasonable plan.

CHAPTER SIX

If I hadn't already made up my mind to go along with Steve's plan, what happened the next day would have been more than enough to convince me.

I was in the living room, doing my best to ignore a conversation between Paige and Anna. That wasn't easy. They were both talking at the same time, which meant the volume kept going up and up. One of their most annoying and least effective communication strategies.

I could have just left the room, but I was there first. Also, I didn't want to give them the satisfaction of driving me out.

Blocking out their nonsense and focusing on my tablet took concentration, so it didn't even register when the phone rang in the other room. Not that I would have paid much attention to the house phone anyway.

The next thing I knew, Mom was hollering my name like I was halfway out of town instead of a few feet down the hall.

"DER-REK!"

I hardly had time to turn my head when she appeared in the archway. Her face was lit with some strange kind of motherly excitement, which immediately caused Paige and Anna to fall silent.

"Call for you, Derek," Mom announced, holding the phone toward me. And then, in the loudest whisper in history, she added, "It's a *girl.*"

"Ooooooooo," said Paige and Anna, as perfectly synchronized as if they'd rehearsed it.

I grabbed the phone and slammed my hand over the mouthpiece — as if it wasn't too late. I tore out of there and raced up the stairs to my room where I could talk without my sisters pretending they weren't listening to every word. As soon as I was inside, I took a deep breath so I wouldn't be panting like some kind of perv when I answered.

"Hello?"

"Derek?"

"Yeah."

"This is Tamrah Kingston."

Yeah, right. There was *no way* Tamrah Kingston was calling me. I snorted good and loud to let this trickster know I wasn't that gullible. Except, as I did that, my brain caught up with the rest of me and I realized, against all odds, it actually *was* Tamrah. Her voice is unmistakable — rich and warm and *definitely* the voice on the other end of the phone.

I did my best to cover the snort by switching to a violent cough.

"Are you okay?" Tamrah asked. She sounded more nervous than concerned.

I quit coughing. Possibly too abruptly.

"I'm fine," I said. "Great, in fact. I just, uh, ate some cayenne."

"By itself?"

Was it my imagination, or had that impressed her? So hard to tell — awe and shock can sound a lot alike.

"I don't do it that often," I said vaguely. Thinking fast isn't my strong point, but claiming to swallow a spoonful of cayenne was dumb even for me. I changed the subject with a witty question.

"So, what's up?"

"I was calling to invite you to a party I'm having on Friday. At my place."

My stupid quota must have been full for the day because I ignored my first instinct, which was to ask: *Why?*

"Great, thanks," I said.

If my sister Kim had received this invitation, she'd have asked a bunch of questions. Did the party have a theme? What would people be wearing? Should they bring something with them? Blah, blah, blah. Her brain is hard-wired to inquire.

I, of course, asked nothing, and it wasn't until I'd hung up that it occurred to me a bit more information might actually be useful. Like, what time.

I shrugged that off. I had days to find out anything I needed to know.

The main thing, and at that moment the *only* thing that mattered was that Tamrah Kingston had called me and asked me to a party.

Of course, I knew *why*. It was the photos. If it wasn't for the photobomb and the picture with Luna Amatulli, the moon would have turned into a gigantic meatball before a girl like Tamrah ever invited me anywhere.

Tamrah Kingston!

Did I mention she was gorgeous? And, while I've never personally gotten very close to her, Steve sits behind her in History and (I hope this won't make you think less of the guy) he's actually told me she *smells* good. He's even used words like citrusy and spicy and, one time, luscious. I remember having the urge to smack him out of it, like a victim of shock.

But after two minutes on the phone with her, I understood that what had happened to Steve really wasn't his fault. I knew this because of the goofy face that was grinning at me idiotically from my dresser mirror.

"That's right," I said, pointing a finger at my reflection. "She wants you bad."

"*Who* wants you?"

I spun around to find Paige smirking at me from the doorway.

"Get out of my room!"

"I'm not *in* your room, I'm in the hall." She nodded toward the phone, still in my hand. "Mom sent me to see if you were done — she has to make a call."

I passed it over and waited just long enough for her to get down the stairs before I followed. Except, I hauled on my shoes and headed for the front door, calling behind me that I was going to Steve's place.

"Supper will be ready at six," Mom said, appearing in the kitchen doorway. "Make sure you're back in time."

I said I would and beat it out of there.

Steve's mom answered the door.

"Oh, hi Derek," she said. "Steve's in his room."

I told her thanks, stepped inside and hurried down the hall to Steve's room. His door was partly open so I shoved it the rest of the way and swaggered in like a guy with something to brag about.

"Hey," Steve said. "What are you doing here?"

"Thought I'd fill you in on something that just happened." I shoved a balled-up sweatshirt off the edge of his desk and leaned against it. He raised an eyebrow and waited.

"Tamrah Kingston just called me."

His eyes actually bugged out.

Then he grinned, like I'd gotten him good.

"Sure she did," he said.

"Seriously. She invited me to a party at her place this Friday."

It took a few minutes, but I finally convinced him I was telling the truth. Which was when he said, "Sweet. This is going to be awesome."

Something uneasy stirred in me.

"I don't know if I'm supposed to bring other people," I said.

"What are you talking about — it's a party. Everyone brings other people."

I hadn't been to a lot of parties. None, in fact, unless you counted Tiffany Manchester's birthday party last year, which she threw for herself. To give you an idea of how cool it was, it featured balloons, streamers and *her mother* hovering around trying to force cake on everyone. (I had four pieces, to be polite.)

But a real party — as in, one that wasn't chaperoned

by a cake-pushing parent? This would be the first. I decided to take Steve's word for what the rules were, even though his social life and mine were pretty much identical.

Chapter Seven

My folks encourage us to bring our friends over. It helps them keep track of where we are and what we're doing. And they like knowing who we're hanging around with.

For me, that's Steve and a couple of other guys.

In Anna's case, I think she'd bring home stray animals if she could, but the friends she has practically fit that category anyway. There's always something scraggly and woebegone about them, as if they were left somewhere on the side of the road.

Paige goes from being a bit of a loner to having a BFF who practically lives here. Until they get mad at each other, which always happens. Then they never speak again as far as I can tell, and she goes back into loner mode until she makes a new BFF. Except the second F never works out.

Kim is the social butterfly in our family. When she's home she's hardly ever alone. Steffie used to be the person who was here with her the most, but lately she's been dragging home that nasty Riley, always with Trisha, a quiet girl who makes me think of shadows. They seemed like an odd combination until the other day when I heard Riley telling Mom she and Trisha are cousins.

"I'm just living at Trisha's place while my mom and dad are working out of the country," she said.

"What do your parents do?" Mom asked.

"They're with Doctors Without Borders," Riley told her. "They spend time in different parts of the world."

"It must be hard on you, having them away like that," Mom said. "When will they be back?"

"I'm not sure," Riley told her. "The dates keep changing."

"At least you're able to be with family," Mom said.

"Right," Riley said, but she didn't sound thrilled. It gave me the impression she didn't like living at her cousin's place all that much.

It was probably because I was paying more attention than usual to who was around that I noticed Junior hadn't been over for a while. That had me thinking Paige might have given up pretending she had a boyfriend. So, naturally, just as it seemed that bit of grossness was over, Junior appeared back on the scene.

It was Thursday, right after supper, when Anna answered the door and found him standing there.

"Oh," she said. "It's you."

"Is Paige home?" he asked.

"Paige!" Anna called out.

"Is that my *boyfriend*?" Paige hollered back from the kitchen. "Tell him to come in."

But Anna told him ... nothing. Most likely she figured if *she'd* heard Paige, then *he* had too, and saw no reason to waste any more of her time on him. Instead, she turned and walked away from the door without a word. I was on the upstairs landing, on my way to the bathroom, but I paused to see what Junior's reaction would be. He stood there looking lost.

I watched with interest as his expression morphed into a kind of worried frown. For a second it looked like he might step inside. He started to put his foot forward, but then he lost his nerve and pulled it back. I swear, I could practically see some of the things he was thinking. Like, where was Paige and why wasn't she coming to his rescue instead of leaving him standing there like a doofus?

Then he noticed me and his face lit up with hope.

"Hi, Derek," he said. "I'm here to see Paige."

"Huh," I answered, and ducked into the bathroom. By the time I came back out, there was a commotion in the living room with Junior in the middle of it. He looked like he wished he'd stayed home. Paige was railing against the mistreatment her fake beloved had received at the hands of her siblings. We were, by Paige's estimation, the WORST brother and sister EVER.

I found myself undisturbed by the label, while Anna looked downright bored. If she'd had another couple of minutes to get it out of her system, Paige's anger would have fizzled out and that would have been the end of it.

Unfortunately, Dad heard the squabbling and came along to intervene. If there's one thing Dad thinks he's really good at, it's squashing squabbles among his kids. His theory (which I've actually heard him tell people) is that diversion is the greatest peacekeeping technique ever. So Dad *diverts*. Usually with a bizarre and sudden change of subject.

It can be pretty jarring.

So there was Paige showing off her limited cache of adjectives, when suddenly, Dad rushed into the room and blurted, "I bet none of you know what a blue moon is."

Junior blinked and looked around like he'd wandered into an alternate universe and was trying to spot a secret passage back to his own planet.

"Uh, a blue moon?" he repeated.

"That's right! I'm sure you've heard the expression 'Once in a blue moon,' but did you ever stop to wonder what a blue moon actually is?" Dad said, sounding a lot like a game show host.

Junior stared harder. "Not really," he said, when it became apparent an answer was expected.

"You've never been curious about it?" Dad asked.

This time, Junior kept quiet. I noticed he seemed to be edging toward the hall, and he might have made a break for it if I hadn't moved to the left and blocked his escape path.

I'm betting it will be a while before he comes here again.

And, oh yeah. It turns out that when there are two full moons in the same month, the second one is called a blue moon. Not the most fascinating thing I've ever heard, but I don't suppose it did me any harm learning that bit of trivia.

CHAPTER EIGHT

Friday came, and everything was nicely set up. As far as Mom and Dad knew, I was going to be hanging out at Steve's place for the evening — an impression I'd managed to give them without actually lying.

They might have said I could go to Tamrah's party if I'd asked, but not without ruining the whole thing for me first. Mom would have called Tamrah's mother and asked a bunch of embarrassing questions. No way I could let that happen.

As soon as supper was over with, I headed to Steve's place. He was home alone, not that it mattered. His mother almost never asks what he's up to. He's got it made, the way he comes and goes and does what he wants without parents watching every move he makes, or sisters running around in various states of crisis.

On the walk to Tamrah's house Steve made a point of sniffing the air and amusing himself with a few wise-cracks about an explosion at a perfume factory. When I didn't react, he came right out and asked what the heck I had on.

"What? This?" I said, trying to sound manly. "Just a bit of aftershave."

"After *what*?"

"Aftershave."

"What'd you shave? Your legs?"

"Ha. Ha," I said, deadpan, though it was kind of funny. It sure cracked Steve up. He was still chuckling when we got to Tamrah's place and turned up the driveway to the side door.

There was a fair amount of noise from inside and I had to ring the doorbell a few times before Tamrah came along, peering through the glass and waving us in. I thought she frowned a little when she saw Steve, but then she smiled and said she was glad we could make it, so I guess it was okay.

We followed her into a room that was half full of kids — mostly from our school. Music blared in the background and it seemed everyone was yelling to be heard over it. One girl was dancing by herself in the middle of the room, turning and swaying and holding her hands up in a fluttery kind of way. I tried not to stare.

Someone noticed me and called out, "Hey, it's the photo guy!"

"Is that what they call you?" a girl I vaguely recognized asked.

"They call me Derek," I said.

"But you're the photo guy, right?" the first person insisted.

"You need a nickname," added the second girl.

The next thing I knew, there were a bunch of nickname suggestions being tossed around. None of them were cool or clever, but I smiled, playing the good sport and hoping none would stick.

It was a relief when the dancing girl jumped on the couch and everyone's attention shifted. By the time she'd finished performing and returned to the floor, the subject of what to call me had been forgotten.

I drifted around the room for a while. These weren't kids I usually hung with, but everyone was friendly enough. It was all laid back and a lot tamer than what I'd expected. Until about an hour later, when something unusual happened.

That was when Tamrah and I had what I can only describe as an encounter. I was coming out of the bathroom when I found myself face to face with her.

"Oh, sorry," I said, because I thought she was waiting to get in there. It turned out she had something else on her mind.

She took my hand and tugged me into a nearby bedroom. Hers, I guess. I didn't exactly take in a lot of details on the decor. Tamrah nudged the door half shut with her foot and stepped closer to me.

"So—" she said.

"So—" I repeated. I wasn't one hundred percent sure what "so" was supposed to mean. (At that moment, I wasn't one hundred percent sure what my name was.) Sweat started to burst out in tiny beads on my forehead.

She leaned in (I'd like to say "up" but the truth is, I haven't had the growth spurt I keep hearing about) closing her eyes and puckering her lips.

My brain slow-processed this information and sent out the message that she was inviting me to kiss her — but something had paralyzed me. (As in, fear.) I stood there, as stiff as a statue.

I'm almost positive I'd have regained the ability to move if we'd made contact — like the Tin Man when he's given oil in *The Wizard of Oz*, but that didn't happen so I'll never know for sure.

After a long moment she opened her eyes, drew back and looked at me. Then she burst out laughing.

"You're hilarious," she said between gasps of glee.

This observation did nothing to improve my comprehension of what was happening. But it was also the exact second I realized something that hadn't registered during my panic the moment before.

Tamrah had been holding up her phone, snapping selfies as she'd stood there, poised and waiting to be kissed.

"What's going on?" I demanded.

"They're for *Strandz*," she said, turning her phone toward me.

What she was showing me was a page on a website some techies from the high school built last year. Its official name is *Breval Strandz*, but everyone just calls it *Strandz*. It features local happenings — the stranger the better as long as they're not actually mean or offensive. The administrators have it set up to protect stuff from being shared outside the site, and you need to be registered and approved to gain access, so it's generally parent-approved.

The page I found myself staring at featured the photobomb of me on the stairs posted next to the picture of me with Luna Amatulli. (Steve had been cropped out.) Underneath these images were these words: *Did the Luna kiss really happen? Sources say no. Now we're looking for a legit photo of Derek giving his first kiss!*

Tamrah giggled and I managed to force out a weak laugh. My head reeled with what I'd just seen.

Her eyes narrowed. "Wait a minute. You already saw this, right?"

"Um, why?" I said uneasily.

"Because if you didn't know, that means you actually didn't *want* to kiss me," she said. "So, which was it?"

"Well, I, uh—"

But Tamrah's attention had shifted again, relieving me of the need to answer. Her thumb was on the screen of her phone and she was flicking back and forth through a half dozen pictures — the ones she'd taken just seconds before.

"Okay, you're in the clear," she announced. "And these are amazing!"

I was having a bit of trouble keeping up.

"Look at this! You *obviously* knew!" she said, smiling widely as she turned the phone around and showed one of the images to me.

And there we were, Tamrah's mouth a whisper away from mine while I stood with my face contorted and my eyes wide and terrified. It looked *exactly* as if I was doing it on purpose.

Photo fluke number three.

Chapter Nine

"Would you stop punching me!"

"Sorry, man." Steve dropped his fist to his side. "It's just that this is all so unbelievable."

"I don't see how pounding my shoulder and calling me 'dawg' makes it easier to believe."

I edged to the far right of the sidewalk, rubbing my upper arm and watching warily for any sign that he might strike again. We were headed home after leaving Tamrah's place and had barely turned the corner when the first blow landed.

"You're missing the point," I said, although I couldn't help feeling just a little smug that the girl who'd inspired my buddy to use the word "luscious" had been willing to let me kiss her.

"Yeah? And exactly what point am I missing?"

"She was only doing it because of that dumb website."

Steve snickered. "So what?" he said. "You think gorgeous girls are ever going to want you to kiss them again?"

He made a weird puckering face, licked his lips and shoved his face toward me. I moved a little further away because some things make you nervous even when you're a hundred percent sure they won't really happen.

"*One* girl," I said.

"One girl *so far*," he said. "That challenge is still out there, bro."

A hunk of lead landed in the pit of my stomach as that thought sank in. Until this thing was over, I'd have to view any girl being friendly to me with suspicion.

It didn't exactly make me feel great.

———

SOMETIMES IT'S HARD to decide which one of my sisters is the biggest pain, but Paige is *definitely* in the lead at the moment.

The thing that bothers me the most is how interested she is in my life. The whole idea of that — start to finish — is a complete mystery to me.

Also, it's totally one-sided. Do *I* bother *her*? Keep track of what she's up to?

No, I do not. Because I couldn't care less.

But Paige seems to have an insane need to stay informed up-to-the-minute on every last thing I'm doing. She noses around until she finds things out and then, believe it or not, she *asks* me about them. Like, I might think, hey, my sister is snooping into my affairs — obviously the smart thing for me to do is help her out, make sure she's got all the information she'll need later on when she's making my life miserable, or ratting me out to my folks, or finding new ways to publicly embarrass me.

At times, it seems like her private mission — her reason for getting up in the morning. So it was no big surprise when she brought up the kiss challenge on Saturday morning.

"Anyone trick you into kissing them yet, or is your homely face enough to keep them away?"

I ignored her, because that strategy might actually work someday.

Kim glanced up from admiring her toenails, which she'd painted bright blue a few minutes earlier.

I opted to slink out of the TV room instead of answering. They followed me to the kitchen.

"So? *Did* you kiss anyone?" Kim asked.

"If you've been on *Strandz*, you should be able to figure it out yourself, genius," I said. I scooped some ice cream into a dish, smashed up a couple of Oreos and sprinkled them on top.

"Only one picture has been sent in so far," Paige said, turning her phone toward Kim to show her the photo Tamrah had submitted, in spite of its lack of a kiss. "It's some girl puckered up, but Derek is messing with her."

"Is that Jacob Kingston's sister?" Kim asked, peering at the picture.

"Yeah," I said, because there are some things a person doesn't mind admitting.

"Where'd this happen?"

"Her place."

"I heard there was a party there last night. Is that when she took this?"

Uh oh.

I shrugged, like talking about the details was starting to bore me. But it was too late.

"I heard you tell Mom you were going to Steve's last night!" Paige said. Her face lit up with joy at the thought that she had something on me.

"So what? Maybe we decided to go to Tamrah's place later."

"*If* that's even true, I bet you didn't phone to let anyone know," Paige said.

We both knew I'd be grounded if I got caught lying, or not keeping Mom posted on where I'd been. She doesn't freak about too many things, but those are big rules at our place.

"Are you actually so bored that you have nothing better to do than bother me?"

Paige smiled her evil sister smile — a natural pose for her. "What's that you're making?" she asked, pointing at my ice cream and cookie combo.

I'd just finished stirring it into a smooth mixture and it looked perfect. Since the look on her face told me what was coming next, I gave the spoon a good lick and stuck it into the middle of the bowl.

"Ice cream with Oreos," I told her. "Want some?"

She gave me a disgusted look and flounced out of the room and down the hall, leaving just Kim and me there.

"Sorry," Kim said.

"For what?" I asked cautiously. An apology that isn't being forced out of her by a parent is a bit rare for Kim.

"I didn't know you snuck to the party. I wouldn't have said anything in front of Miss Blabbermouth."

Unlike the family blackmailer whose silence can be bought, Paige was the type who might get in some minor bit of trouble and rat me out to take the pressure off herself.

All I could do was hope for the best. Not that I had a lot of options. Besides, there were a few things I needed to get done before meeting up with Steve.

We'd decided to check out the animal shelter after lunch. And considering what happened yesterday, I thought the sooner we did that, the better. With any luck and the cooperation of a few kittens, we'd have some new photos in no time.

CHAPTER TEN

The woman behind the desk at the animal shelter looked at me and Steve like we were covered in fleas and had dropped in to spread them to the animals. Even Steve seemed a bit unnerved as he stepped up to a ledge that looked into her office.

She rolled her chair back, stood up and came over.

"What can I do for you boys?"

Her voice was a surprise. It was warm and friendly, and it was followed by a smile that transformed her completely.

"I called the other day," Steve said. "About the animals."

"Yes?"

"Are you the person I was talking to?" Steve asked.

"Possibly," she said, now looking amused. "We get a lot of calls — about the animals. Were you interested in adopting?"

"Uh, no. We just wanted to spend some time with

them. The lady I was talking to said we needed to fill in a form."

"For volunteering, then," she said. She looked back and forth between me and Steve. "You both want to volunteer?"

We nodded and she produced two copies of a form from a filing cabinet and pushed them toward us, along with a couple of pens.

"There's a visitor's room around the corner if you'd like to sit down to fill those in."

"This place smells bad," I hissed under my breath as we slid into chairs in the visitor's room.

"It's all the animal poop," Steve said.

"Oh, thanks. I'd never have figured that out on my own."

We got busy filling in the forms, which had questions on both sides of the page. I was thinking it was kind of a bother for the sake of a few pictures, especially since we wouldn't be coming back after that.

Then a chocolate brown puppy ran skidding and tumbling into the room, followed by a couple of giggling girls. I recognized them as Sharon and Denise, who are in our grade at school.

"Oh!" Sharon said, stopping short when she saw that the room wasn't empty. "Steve, right? And the famous

Derek Cowell, of course."

I couldn't help feeling a bit of an ego surge. People who used to call me Darren or Rick or other names that aren't mine, now knew I was Derek Cowell. From "invisible" to "famous" just like that. Not that I took the famous part seriously.

"Hey! Come here, you," Denise said.

I cringed. Not another girl trying to lure me over to kiss her! Then I realized she was talking to the puppy. She scooped it into her arms where it wriggled and squirmed and began licking her face madly.

"Dunlop!" she scolded cheerfully. "You behave yourself."

Dunlop paused, yawned widely, and kept right on doing puppy things.

"Cute dog," Steve said. "Are you adopting him?"

"I wish!" Denise answered. "My sister is allergic, but I get my furry fix volunteering here every weekend."

"Is that why you guys are here?" Sharon asked. "To volunteer?"

The question wasn't really necessary since she was gawking at the papers on the table, but Steve never misses a chance to impress girls.

"We sure are," he said. "We hope to make these help-less creatures' lives a little better."

"If we'd known that, we would have saved some of the boring jobs for you," Denise said.

"Such as?"

"Cleaning, laundry, sorting food donations — that kind of thing."

"Actually, we're just here to play with kittens," I said. Steve elbowed me, nearly shoving me off the chair.

"Always the jokester," he said, shaking his head ruefully. "We'll do whatever we can to help."

"True animal lovers," Denise said with a happy sigh.

"That pretty much describes us," Steve agreed.

"Well, we'd better let you get back to your paperwork, or you might not have time for your interviews today," Sharon said.

"Say bye-bye to the nice boys now," Denise said. She made Dunlop wave his paw, and the three of them disappeared out the doorway and out of sight. I turned to Steve.

"What interviews?" I asked.

"I didn't mention that?"

"No. You did *not* mention that. And what kind of questions would you need to ask a person who's offering to volunteer at an animal shelter? 'Do you know who Lassie is?' 'Have you ever watched *101 Dalmatians*?'"

"I didn't know Sharon volunteered here," Steve said in

a faraway voice. It was like he hadn't heard a word I'd just said.

A few minutes later we were passing the completed forms over and being ushered into the office.

"I'm Gabriel Dawson — everyone calls me Gabby," the woman we'd met earlier said, shaking hands first with Steve and then with me. She pointed us into chairs. "Now, tell me why you want to volunteer at the shelter."

"We like animals," said Steve.

"Right," I agreed.

"And what do you know about our work here?"

"You take care of cats and dogs and other pets that have no homes — until they get adopted," Steve said. "My mom got our dog Slipper here. Only, his name wasn't Slipper then."

She asked a few questions about that, and then wanted to know if we had any experience in caring for animals. I let Steve do most of the talking.

The interview lasted about fifteen minutes, and it must have gone well because at the end of it Gabby told us they'd be happy to have us help. She said there was always lots of work to do at the shelter and made it sound as if that was something for us to get excited about. Then she told us we could start anytime we liked.

"How about now?" Steve asked.

"Perfect," Gabby said. But before we could mention the kitten room, she grabbed a couple of leashes and led us outside to the kennels.

"The dogs *love* a chance to go for a walk," she said as she hooked up the collars of the two biggest dogs.

"This is Dutch," she told Steve as she passed him one leash. And then, giving me the other, "And this is Pepper."

Dutch and Pepper were jumping, barking and trembling with excitement during the introductions. After that, they launched into an impromptu crotch-sniffing contest which I'm pretty sure Pepper won.

The next thing we knew, we were nearly jerked off our feet while Dutch and Pepper raced down the road with us in tow. I barely managed to stay upright and Steve didn't seem to be doing much better as this maniacal pair of canines tore along, dragging us behind them.

They ran in and out of private yards while we called out commands for them to stop, slow down, heel and anything else we could think of. I believe it's safe to say they finished at the bottom of the class in obedience school.

It wasn't until they'd rushed about whizzing on every bush and power pole within a couple of blocks that they slowed enough for us to catch our breath and work our shoulders back into their sockets.

Back at the shelter at last, we were told how excited

the other dogs were. Apparently, any time one or two of them get taken out, the rest think they're going to have turns too.

"I know you won't want to disappoint them," Gabby said.

That's *exactly* what I wanted to do and I was about to say so when Sharon and Denise came outside. The second he saw the girls, Steve announced loudly that we'd be more than happy to take every dog in the country for a walk if that's what was needed.

By the time we finished our volunteering for the day, my legs had turned to rubber and there were more nose-prints on my crotch than I wanted to think about.

We hadn't even *seen* the kitten room.

CHAPTER ELEVEN

Going back to school on Monday was like walking into an alternate reality.

As far as I could tell, every last student had seen the picture of Tamrah leaning toward me, lips puckered and eyes closed dreamily, in sharp contrast to mine, which were bugged out in apparent shock and terror.

I heard the word "genius" constantly. Unlike any other occasion that word had crossed my path, this time it was in reference to me — Derek Cowell. The thought that I hadn't been posing — that I had, in fact, actually *been* shocked and terrified — didn't seem to occur to anyone. Instead, the new picture cemented my standing as a guy with unusual comedic ability and timing.

The admiration was the upside. Unfortunately, there was a downside too. The *other* thing was the crazy amount of interest in the sought-after kiss.

As the days passed, I couldn't go anywhere without hearing kissing sounds. A few girls made clumsy attempts to trick me into the desired shot, but I easily drove them off with spirited bouts of coughing and sneezing.

This all probably sounds amusing. It wasn't. The first two days didn't bother me much, but when there was no sign of things easing up by day three, it was seriously starting to gross me out. Plus my throat was getting sore from all the fake coughing.

Who wants to be eyeballed like a prize cupcake?

It didn't end there either. There were plenty of snickers and whispers too, not to mention actual, out loud comments. Some of the things I heard were creepy, even disturbing.

It was almost enough to make me wish I could go back to being Derek the invisible.

Steve was not helpful. Actually, I have to say that he was the *opposite* of helpful. He made no effort to hide how hilarious he found my predicament, and couldn't seem to grasp how awkward it made me feel.

Instead, he continuously urged me to take advantage of what was probably (according to him) going to be my only chance to kiss a girl in the foreseeable future.

Obviously, there was no way I could get him to understand that I had zero — maybe *less* than zero — interest in kissing anyone, no matter how attractive she was, no matter how willing she seemed, when her motivation had nothing to do with liking me.

"You aren't being very supportive," I grumbled at one point.

For a second, Steve stared at me like I'd spoken in code and he was trying to decipher it. Then he howled with laughter.

So, yeah, Steve totally failed in that department.

By Friday I was fed up with the whole thing. That was the day Janine Labelle, one of the girls who'd made a failed attempt to lure me into a kiss earlier in the week, decided to get revenge. She and a couple of her friends were waiting at my locker when I got to school that morning. The way they started giggling the second they saw me told me something was up, but it wasn't until I got closer that I found out what.

I stopped dead in my tracks. For a couple of seconds, I just stood there staring at Janine's shirt. (Not *that* way — I'm not a jerk.) Staring right back was a close-up of *me*, obviously taken on the sly. It was not a flattering picture.

The blown-up shot of my mug was bad enough, but the caption was worse.

It said: GERM FACTORY

Of course, the school has a dress code. Janine would never have been allowed to walk around openly wearing something like that. But she came prepared. Anytime a teacher was within sight, she zipped up the hoodie she'd been smart enough to wear over top of the T-shirt.

Everyone thought it was a hoot. Well, almost everyone.

It was a long day, but it finally ended.

I was out the door and on my way home seconds after the last bell. Steve and I usually walk together so I knew he'd be wondering why I'd ducked him, but I didn't care. I was in desperate need of a few minutes alone to clear my head.

Then I heard my name being called and realized someone was running behind me. When I turned, I saw it was Denise.

"Wait up!" she called.

My first instinct was to take off, but she looked so determined I was pretty sure she'd catch me. That made me wonder what she wanted, which led to the ever-present worry about the stupid kiss challenge.

By the time she reached me I had my hand firmly clapped over my mouth, as a kind of signal that I had no intentions of kissing her. To be extra safe, I took a backward step.

"What's wrong with you?" she asked.

"What's wrong with *you*?" I demanded.

"*What*? Move your hand — I can't make out what you're saying."

"You'd like that wouldn't you?" I scoffed. In a muffled kind of way.

She frowned for a couple of seconds, shrugged and said, "I don't know what your problem is, but anyway, I have an idea."

I listened as she explained. By the time she was halfway through, I'd dropped my hand to my side. There was a kiss involved all right, but it wasn't with her.

"I don't know," I said slowly. "It *might* work."

"Of course it will work," Denise insisted. Clearly, *she* thought it was a good idea and saw no reason to give me time to think it over.

Not that it was a bad idea. What I'd grasped of it as she'd raced through the details sounded okay. I just don't like to rush into anything.

If Denise registered my hesitation, she didn't let on.

"Okay, so let's go."

"What? Now?"

She didn't even bother answering that, unless you count an impatient wave for me to get moving.

Five minutes later we were at the shelter and Gabby was ushering us into the visitor room where Steve and I had filled out our applications. A few things had been rearranged to create a background for picture taking.

"I'll go get Skylah," Gabby said, hurrying into the hallway.

"It looks like you had this all set up before you asked me," I said pointedly.

Denise smiled and said, "I knew you'd want to help." I noticed she didn't meet my eyes.

Gabby was back in no time. She had a black and white cat in her arms.

"Skylah is shy, so she may be a bit resistant to a stranger holding her," she told me.

"Aren't there any friendly cats?" I asked.

"Sure there are, but this one has been here longer than most," Denise explained. "So she's the best choice."

"How long has she been here?" I asked.

"About a year."

"A year!" I echoed. I'd assumed the animals at the shelter all got homes within a month or two.

"We're a no kill shelter," Gabby told me. "We house them as long as it takes. That means there are always a lot of cats, and the ones who are shy or fearful sometimes wait a long time for a home."

A second later Denise had her phone out, ready to start snapping pictures. "Okay, go!" she said and Gabby passed Skylah over to me.

Just as Gabby had predicted, the cat was not thrilled

to find herself being held by someone she didn't know. She made a low, growling sound in her throat while I did my best to calm her, talking in a soft, friendly voice, which Denise had promised would help. It didn't seem to. As I moved closer to Skylah her front paws came up in an aggressively defensive pose. She hissed and leaned backward away from me.

"I think she likes you," Denise said drily.

By the time the photo shoot was over, the cat had bent herself into some pretty creative shapes trying to avoid me. For the most part, she was successful, but with some effort I got close enough for the picture Denise was after. My reward for this was a scratch on the chin and a fair amount of what I figured was cat cussing.

I was only too happy to pass the creature back to Gabby, who managed to keep a straight face and ask me if she should get out adoption papers.

"I think I'll wait until the bleeding stops," I told her, while Denise dabbed at my chin with a tissue.

Gabby insisted on spraying it with some kind of cat germ killer which she squirted at my wound like a madwoman.

"This might sting a bit," she said.

It didn't. It stung a lot.

CHAPTER TWELVE

As soon as I got home I made a beeline for the bathroom. In spite of (or maybe because of) Gabby's spray, the cat scratch was red and angry. I rubbed some white ointment from the medicine cabinet on it until it was hardly noticeable.

When I went back downstairs Dad was just pulling into the driveway. He tapped the horn before he got out of the car, which is a signal for one of us to go help him bring stuff in. It's usually me because, for some odd reason, the girls never hear the horn.

"Mom's working a bit late so I'll be the chef tonight," he said, passing me a couple of bags to carry.

Considering some of the meals my dad has produced, I'm not sure he actually knows what a chef is. But, my philosophy is, if there's going to be food, I'm good.

"Cool," I said. "What are you making?"

"Thought I'd light the old barbeque and throw on some burgers and a few of those fat, spicy sausages."

Dad doesn't like to say "Italian" sausages. He thinks it sounds like an ethnic slur.

"Want some help getting stuff ready?" I offered. Anything to get the food on the table quicker. So, I ended up forming ground beef into patties, slicing tomatoes and dill pickles and setting out the ketchup and other condiments while Dad lit the barbeque and got ready to start grilling.

I like my dad.

That might sound like a weird comment to make out of the blue, but it's true and I felt like saying it. He's a good guy.

"Dad made barbeque," I told Mom when she got home. She smiled and sniffed the air with the happy face of someone who doesn't care what's for dinner as long as she doesn't have to make it.

"Should I set an extra place?" Paige asked. "Is Kim's friend staying?"

That was something I'd been wondering too. Or, actually, I'd been wondering which friend was over. I'd heard voices in her room and was hoping it might be Steffie, but short of going up there and pressing my ear against her door, there was no way to find out. (I might even have done that if I'd been sure I wouldn't get caught, but that is *not* the way my luck tends to lean.)

Mom sent Paige up to find out and a few minutes later when she came back, Kim was behind her. My mood took a nose-dive when I saw that the person with her was Riley.

Mom asked her if she wanted to stay for dinner.

"Um, maybe," Riley said slowly, like she needed to think about whether or not she could do Mom this favor. "What are you having?"

When she heard it was burgers and Italian sausages, Riley's lip curled in disgust. "Is there a gluten-free, vegan option?" she asked.

"Riley doesn't eat animal products. Or gluten," Kim added, as if we needed that explained.

"In case you're wondering, the sausages aren't actually made of Italians," I said helpfully.

"Ignore him, Riley," Kim said. "As you've probably noticed, he's a moron."

Dad chose that exact moment to come through the patio door with his meat-laden tray. "Another delicious dinner by Chef Dad," he announced. Then, spying Riley, he added. "Oh, a guest. Hello there."

Riley gave him a stiff nod and averted her eyes from the sizzling burgers and sausages he was transferring to a platter on the table.

"Thanks for inviting me, but I think I'd better go

home," she said, fading toward the doorway like a vampire avoiding the light.

Supper was amazing. Chef quality, even. The only thing that kept me from enjoying it one hundred percent was the thing I heard Anna mutter under her breath as Riley went out the door.

"Well, it's not *her*, that's for sure."

Which told me I'd been right. She *had* suspected the truth about the stairway photobomb. It was only a matter of time before she figured out which girl had been the cause of my sappy-stunned look that day.

CHAPTER THIRTEEN

I'm not exactly sure why, but I didn't tell Steve about the picture Denise took of me and Skylah. Which meant he found out the same time everyone else did, less than twenty-four hours later, when photo number four made its way to the *Strandz* site.

He was not pleased when he showed up at my place the next afternoon. Even his knock sounded angry.

"Hi," I said, letting him in. He threw me a quick glare, but didn't answer and I watched as he stomped past me and straight up the stairs to my room. That was my second hint there was a problem.

I trudged along behind him dragging my feet and feeling a bit like a prisoner on his way to the gallows. Steve had turned to face me by the time I entered the room. His fists were white balls at his side and although I knew he'd never hit me — not seriously anyway — I kept my distance just to be sure.

"You want to tell me what you think you're doing?"

I tried to look puzzled when I said, "You mean about the picture?"

"Yeah, Derek, I mean about the picture."

"It was Denise's idea," I said.

"She overpowered you, did she? Twisted your arm?" Steve said, but he didn't wait for an answer. He whipped out his phone and slid his thumb over the surface. A tap or two later and he'd brought up the offending image. I'd seen it earlier, but I stepped closer and leaned in for another look. The sight almost made me smile, but I managed to hold it back. Barely.

"Challenge met," Steve said, reading the caption below the picture.

The grin got loose and I put my hand over my mouth like I was in a state of serious concentration.

Steve scowled and scrolled down to the brief write-up underneath the photo, which he read out loud.

"Sorry, girls — Derek's first kiss has been claimed by Skylah the cat. She's being smooched by the local photo star here at the animal shelter where she's been living for more than a year. Although Skylah has won Derek's heart, she's still waiting for her forever home."

He didn't bother reading the rest of it, which talked about how sad life was for the cats that get passed over. It also gave adoption information for Skylah, for anyone who might be interested.

"*Denise* thought it up," I said, in case he'd missed that point the first time.

She'd taken an absolutely brilliant picture too — snapped at the perfect second.

Skylah was standing on her hind legs with her paw on my cheek, which made it seem as if she was trying to push me away. My eyes were closed, but the cat's were wide and wild in alarm. It was like a reverse of the picture of Tamrah trying to get kissed, except, of course, the girl in this shot was a cat.

Steve sighed and shoved his phone back into his pocket. "You realize this totally messes up the plan with the kittens," he said.

"Why?"

"Because, obviously everyone will think we got the idea from *this*."

I knew immediately that he was right. "Sorry," I said.

"Are you?"

"What do you mean, *am I*? What kind of question is that?"

"Well, what would you think if you were me?"

"What are you getting at?" I asked, maybe just a bit too quickly. "You think I'm cutting you out on purpose?"

"It sure looks that way."

"That's crazy," I said.

"Right. And that's why you kept quiet about it too — because it was all so innocent."

"It only happened yesterday," I pointed out.

"You mean when you dodged me after school?"

I stood there for a minute, trying to come up with something to say, which is not exactly my specialty under pressure. But, suddenly, I was mad too.

"You know what, if that's what you want to think, go right ahead," I told him.

Steve looked startled. To be honest, I was kind of startled myself. We stared at each other for what seemed like a long time. Then he moved, fast and hard toward the door, shoving past me on his way out.

I hate arguing. Tension twisted my gut as I heard him pound down the stairs.

We've had arguments before where Steve has started to leave, but he's never made it outside. I waited, listening for the front door. A minute, maybe two, passed and then there it was — the creak of hinges. He was really going this time.

My jaw stiffened in anger. If he wanted to act like a jerk, I sure wasn't going to worry about it. For a second, I wished my window looked out over the front of the house so I could open it and yell some clever insult before he got out of hearing range.

I was imagining how he'd react to that when the door creaked again. Steve hadn't made it off the front step.

My breath expelled in slow relief as I heard footsteps mount the stairs, slower and more subdued than the ones that had descended a moment earlier. I kept my eyes straight ahead as the door opened and his head popped in.

"S'up?" he asked.

I laughed as a grin broke across his face and he shoved the door wide and sauntered in.

"You're the worst bluffer in history," I said.

"I'm never bluffing," he said. "I just get over things fast. But whatever — I have a better idea anyway."

"A better idea for a picture?"

"Not exactly."

"Then what?" I was starting to feel a little uneasy. When Steve takes his time getting to the point, it usually means I'm not going to like it.

This time was no different.

Chapter Fourteen

Steve insisted I would best appreciate his new idea if he could show me what he was talking about. We set off a few minutes later, heading toward the south side of town.

"So, before we get there I'll give you the basic plan," he said when we'd gone a block in silence.

"Okay," I said.

A couple of minutes went by before he spoke again.

"Okay, so first, you have to promise you're not going to be a humongous chicken about this."

"What size chicken *can* I be?"

Steve snickered. He stopped walking and turned to face me. Maybe he thought his suggestion was so shocking I'd pass out right there on the sidewalk, and he'd have to save me from banging my chicken face on the curb.

"This is something totally original," he said.

"Do I have to lay an egg? Because I don't think I'm equipped for it."

Steve ignored that. I could see by the glint in his eye he was psyched about this idea of his and didn't want to waste any more time joking around.

"Skywalking," he said, like that would mean something to me. It didn't.

"Never heard of it."

"I know! That's the whole point. Like I just said, it's totally original."

"That *is* original," I agreed.

And then, I hated to bring him down when he was so charged up, but I felt compelled to point something out.

"You *do* know you can't actually walk in the sky, right?" I said.

"That's what's going to make this so amazing."

Sometimes it's hard to tell when Steve is serious. This was definitely making me wonder. I waited for him to say more, but he wasn't quite ready yet.

"Come on," he said. "It will be better if I show you."

I have to admit my curiosity was growing as we made our way deeper into town, down along Front Street, past the specialty shops and cafes and on to the old train tracks that have been out of use for years. He stopped abruptly in front of the boarded-up train station.

"This is it. The perfect place," he said. I noticed he still wasn't rushing to give me a whole lot of details.

I looked around doubtfully. Aside from the tired stone of the abandoned station and the uncared-for grass and shrubs that surrounded it, there wasn't much to see. Certainly nothing that would have made a good background for a photo shoot.

"The perfect place for what?" I asked.

"Skywalking, of course."

"Right!" I said, whacking him on the back like we were sharing a big joke. He took a large unplanned step forward, waving his arms in circles to catch his balance.

"Hey," he said. "What'd you do that for?"

"I thought you might take off. You know, and do some skywalking."

Steve rolled his eyes. "You can't do it here," he said. Which was when I noticed the way his chin was turned up, and when I followed the angle of his gaze I found myself looking at the roof of the train station.

There was *no way* I was getting on that roof.

This isn't easy to admit, but I have acrophobia, which means I'm afraid of heights. No, afraid isn't a strong enough word. I'm terrified at the very *thought* of heights. I avoid exhibition rides if they're more than a few feet off the ground and I nearly barf when I see someone skydiving out of a plane on television.

You'd think that Steve, being my best friend, would know this. He doesn't. Because I've worked hard to hide my fear from everyone, him included.

"Count me out," I said. "This place is ancient. The roof could be rotten."

"It's not," he said. "It's as solid as can be."

"You were up there?"

"Yep. Last night, when I had the idea. And it's perfect."

"How'd you get in?"

"There's an old coal door into the basement around the other side. One jiggle and the padlock pulled out of the old wood."

He kept talking, but I was busy thinking about how I was going to get out of this without admitting how petrified I was at the thought of being on the roof.

"The problem is, I have that inner ear thing," I said, offering my standby excuse. "But you can go ahead — it sounds cool."

"I knew you'd say that," Steve told me. He stretched his arm out, pointing toward one part of the station's roof. "But there's a flat section."

"So? It's still up in the air." My stomach did a nauseating flip.

"Yeah, but there's no slope on that part, so even if you got dizzy you couldn't fall off," Steve said. "We don't need to be near the edge — we could film from the middle of the flat part."

I found myself wondering if it could work. My acrophobia really only kicks in when I look down. Maybe if I couldn't see over the edge of the roof, I'd be okay.

Steve was watching me closely. He could tell I was wavering.

"Here's what I'm thinking. Remember those clear Plexiglas cubes my mom brought home from her job last year?"

I only took a second to picture the cubes he was talking about. There'd been a dozen or more, all a uniform size of about twenty inches square.

"Those things that were piled in your living room for weeks?"

"Exactly. Mom was going to use them for organizing stuff, but she never got around to it."

"So where are they now?"

"In the basement."

"And?"

"And they're clear. As in, see-through."

"Yeah, I'm familiar with the properties of 'clear.'" I said.

"So, picture this — it will be a video."

"Taken by—?"

"We'll find someone," he said. "It will be dusk out — with the moon just showing up, and we'll be up there, walking around in the sky, *above* the roof."

"On the Plexiglas cubes," I said.

"Exactly."

"I think they'd probably be visible in the video," I said.

"Not if there's a little fog or mist."

"That might work," I said. It did sound cool, and I was talking myself into believing I could handle being up there as long as it was flat, and I didn't look down.

At the same time, I figured I'd better leave myself an out, in case I needed one when the time actually came.

"And anyway, if I can't do it — because of my ear thing — you can go ahead."

"Except it will get more attention if you're in it," Steve said. He sounded as if that was something unpleasant I'd just forced him to admit.

I knew he was right. The recent postings on *Strandz* had turned me into a pretty popular guy.

Besides, my confidence was growing. Probably because my feet were still flat on the ground at that moment.

So I agreed to do it.

CHAPTER FIFTEEN

You know how cars have mirrors that say objects are closer than they appear? Well, being on the outside of things can make them seem a lot more fun and interesting than they really are.

Being in the spotlight had transported me to the other side of the social wall. I was in, and that was great, but there were things I didn't like so much. For example, the feeling that I was being watched — and judged — so much of the time.

That might have been why there was a sense of unease in me at school the next week even though the cat kiss picture had elevated my social status another couple of notches. Mostly because it did what Denise had hoped for — something I, quite frankly, had barely given a thought.

She told me about it at lunchtime, waving at me from across the cafeteria and hurrying over to show me a picture of a young couple holding a cat. Her face was pink and flushed, her eyes bright and shining. It made her look kind of cute.

"Look!" she said, thrusting her phone at me.

"Hmm," I said. I had no idea what her point was as I looked down at a picture of smiling strangers holding a cat.

"It worked!" she told me. "This is Skylah's new family."

I looked closer, as if I was double-checking that the cat in the picture was really Skylah. Not that I'd have been able to tell the difference if it wasn't. One black and white cat looks pretty much like any other black and white cat to me.

"That's great," I said.

"And that's not all," she said excitedly. "Two more cats who have been waiting ages for their forever homes were adopted too."

"That's great," I said again. Denise didn't seem to notice I'd turned into a human echo.

"Okay, so I've gotta go," she said in a sort of dreamy, happy voice. "I just wanted to tell you the awesome news about Skylah and the others."

Word of these adoptions spread like an uncontained fire. And by the end of the day, when I got to my locker, I was *swarmed*.

Swarmed by *girls*, that is. (I'd have been a whole lot less excited if it had been bees.)

Girls to my left, girls to my right, crowded around me, leaning in, smiling, talking. It was enough to make a guy dizzy. In a good way.

They all seemed to be chattering at the same time, but the messages got through in spurts and blurts. I was amazing, the saver of cats' lives, the kind of guy who didn't mind putting himself out there for something he believed in. I, Derek Cowell, was a true animal lover and all round wonderful human being.

No one said a word about Denise's part in the whole thing. I decided it was only right to set the record straight.

"It wasn't *all* me," I said, trying to be heard over the din of praise. "I had help, you know."

"He's so humble," someone else declared. And the whole lot of them let out admiring murmurs.

"He's the *real* hero," said someone from behind me. There was more nodding and agreeing with that, as though I'd won first place in some vague contest.

I made a serious effort to look humble and as I did, my eye was caught by Steve's amused face watching the whole scene from a few feet away. I grabbed what I needed from my locker and edged my way toward him through the cluster of girls.

A moment later he turned to me on the sidewalk, a Grinch-like grin spread across his face. "Is this unbelievable or what?" he asked.

I laughed. "I'd have gone around kissing cats long ago if I'd known this was going to happen," I said.

"And it's a perfect build-up for our skywalking video!" he said. "The more popular *you* get, the more views *it* will get."

The skywalking plan! My enthusiasm took an instant dive and ended in a crash landing. After I'd agreed to do the roof thing, I'd researched a few things about acrophobia.

My hope had been to find out how I could get over it, but what I'd learned was *not* encouraging. The condition has no quick fixes. There *are* things a person can do, but they take time and I didn't have years, or even months, to get ready.

I'd known from the start that the longer I waited, the harder it was going to be to get out of this crazy video idea. The problem was Steve. He was psyched, talking about the progress he was making getting things organized and ready.

He'd never have believed the truth at that point even if I *had* come clean. Who would? It would look as if I was inventing a phobia to get out of sharing the lime-light with him.

There might have been a time when I could have said, "Look, man, I can't. That's all. I just can't."

But it was way too late for that.

Apparently, I was going to have to find a way to get on that roof.

CHAPTER SIXTEEN

I landed home in a bad frame of mind, worried about the train station plan and still drawing a blank on how I could extract myself from it. Engrossed in those thoughts, it barely registered that Anna was slinking up to me. It wasn't until she spoke that she got my attention.

"So, did you have a good time at *the party* you went to?"

I froze, wondering how she'd found out, and waiting to see what the little gangster was going to demand this time. But she never got a chance to tell me, because Mom's voice in the hall stopped that extortion scheme in its tracks.

"What *party*? What is she talking about, Derek?"

Busted.

The way Anna's face crumpled you'd have thought *she* was the one in trouble. I narrowed my eyes at her and drew a finger across my throat, although I had to drop my hand in mid slash when Mom appeared in the doorway. Switching from a threatening glare to an innocent face, I turned my attention to Mom.

"Oh, right. Steve and I were bored, so we went to this girl's place for a bit."

"You went to a party," she said. Only, the way she said it sounded as if I'd done something sinister, like knocking down an old lady and stealing her purse.

"Kind of."

"You don't 'kind of' go to a party," Mom said.

I looked down at the floor and mumbled, "Sorry."

Mom crossed her arms in front of her. Never a good sign. I braced myself for a grounding, which didn't take long coming.

"You can be sorry this weekend," Mom said. "No phone, no computer and no leaving the house."

Trying for a lighter sentence is always worth a shot, and I'd have done that if Kim and Steffie hadn't come through the front door just then. There's no way to look manly when you're begging for mercy, so I dropped it and headed to my room until supper.

Steffie stayed and ate with us, which is pretty common at our house. Not that *she's* here a lot, but that someone is. Mom has this philosophy that if anyone extra is around when we're about to eat, we set another place at the table and make them welcome. She says it's the kind of hospitality she grew up with and she hopes we'll carry the tradition on someday. The girls all say they will. I find that hard to believe considering the way I've seen them act when someone uses a few drops of nail polish or a swipe of lip balm without their permission.

Steffie was sitting right across from me at supper, which was both good and bad. It made it easier for me to look at her without being obvious about it, but she was also more likely to notice if I did something my sisters would describe as gross. That's a long list and it's hard to keep track of everything on it.

As soon as grace was said Steffie gave me a sweet smile and said, "So, any new photos we should watch for?"

Something weird happened in my gut — something silent, thankfully. The fact that Steffie was paying attention to stuff about *me* — I could barely process information that cool. It made me ridiculously happy, but it also made me forget she'd just asked me a question.

"Not saying, huh?" she said after giving me a few more seconds to answer. "I should have known that would be top secret information."

"Yes," I said. "It is."

"So, what's it like being famous?"

I put my brain to work formulating an answer that wouldn't make me sound like: a.) an egomaniac or, b.) someone who grew up speaking gibberish. Which is when Paige jumped in.

"*Derek*, famous? Puh-lease." She followed this with the satisfied look of someone who's just made an incredibly clever remark.

"That's enough of that, Paige," Mom said mildly.

"What did I do?" Paige whined. An attractive sound which she followed up by sticking out her tongue.

"I don't know about the rest of you," Dad jumped in with his jolly change-the-subject voice. "But I sure am looking forward to spending some time at the lake this summer!"

That startled us into silence, which meant my chance for a witty yet modest answer to Steffie's question had passed. I snagged a drumstick, remembering just in time to use my fork instead of grabbing it with my fingers (although what's wrong with that I'll never know) scooped some potatoes and broccoli onto my plate and started to eat.

Conversation was going on around me, but I'd drifted away from it, distracted by the cute way Steffie's nose twitched when she was chewing. Not that I risked looking too often. I knew Anna was still trying to figure out which girl I'd been goofy-faced over in the stairway photobomb.

But then it hit me that Anna didn't have her nosy hawk-eyes trained on me. She was picking at her dinner with her head down and, when I looked a bit closer, I saw that her eyes were filling. Mom saw it too.

"Anna, is something wrong?" she asked.

Anna slowly lifted her face toward Mom. She shook her head "no" which jolted a couple of tears free. They rolled down her cheeks and past her quivering mouth.

By then everyone was looking at her. Dad reached over and patted her hand.

"You want to tell your old dad what's bothering you?" he said.

"I got Derek in trouble," she answered, and then burst into full-blown blubbering.

"What for?" Paige asked. She seemed a lot more interested in that than in Anna's distress.

"I went to a party at Tamrah Kingston's house the other Friday," I said.

That was when Anna rushed to my side and grabbed me around the neck, making a strange wailing sound. The next thing I knew her tear-soaked face was pressing against mine.

"It's okay," I told her. "Calm down already."

"I'm *really* sorry," she howled into my ear. Because nothing says "Sorry" like nearly deafening a person.

"She feels so bad," Steffie said. (When one of my sisters points out something obvious like that, I find it annoying, but in Steffie's case, it seemed kind of cute.)

"Yeah, well—" I looked at Anna doubtfully. Specifically, looked into the wet cavern of her wailing yap.

I'd have liked to shove her soggy, noisy self away and get back to my chicken, but that was out of the question with Steffie looking on. So I put an arm around the little monster, patted her on the back and forced out soothing brotherly words.

"For goodness sakes, Anna," Mom said. "He's only grounded for the weekend, it's not the end of the world."

Anna gulped and swallowed and took a few big breaths and finally got herself under control. From blackmailer to this ... it was just plain weird.

Except, it didn't end there. Something equally strange happened then. Something that had never happened before.

Kim started pleading my case.

"Aw, Mom, that's not fair. Plus it's going to encourage Anna to be a big squealer."

My heart began to fill with gratitude for her sisterly concern and kindness. (Okay, that didn't actually happen.) What my heart actually filled with was suspicion, because there was no way Kim was leaping to my defense unless she had some kind of ulterior motive.

Mom was staring at Kim. She seemed equally mysti-fied at this odd turn of events. Then Kim got to the point.

"Besides, Steffie needs Derek's help this weekend."

"Doing what?" Mom asked, although it seemed to me that was a question *I* should have been asking.

Kim launched into what I can only describe as speed-talk. All of my sisters are accomplished at this particular form of communication, which consists of spewing out sentences faster than the human brain can possibly process them.

In spite of that, I managed to grasp enough details to understand that Kim was invited to go somewhere with Steffie's family on the weekend. Apparently, that left them with no one to take care of the dog, since Kim usually dog-sits for Steffie's family.

"We were having the hardest time trying to come up with a sitter for Boodles," Kim told Mom.

"And then we thought … Derek!" Steffie added. "Now that he's become such an animal lover."

"Well, unfortunately Derek has gotten himself grounded this weekend," Mom said.

And it looked like that was that. Except, it wasn't.

I don't know if it was Anna or Kim or the fact that this seemed to be Unusual Events Day at the Cowell house, but when my folks went to the kitchen to get dessert, they came back to the table with an announcement.

"Derek, your mother and I have decided not to ground you this weekend," Dad said as he sat a bowl of fresh pineapple chunks on the table.

"Seriously?" I asked, looking past the pineapple to a plate of date squares Mom was carrying.

"You'll have an extra chore for a week instead," Mom told me.

Not thrilling, but better than being stuck in the house all weekend.

"Thanks," I said.

"Yay!" Kim said. "Now you can take care of Boodles after all!"

My head snapped up and I found myself looking directly into Steffie's eyes, which were lit up and shining.

"*Would* you, Derek?" she asked.

"What do I have to do?" I asked, knowing very well I'd never say no to her. I focused on her eyes and tried to block out the thought of another slobbering, pawing canine whose poop I'd have to collect like I was on some kind of bizarre treasure hunt.

"Just go over to the house to feed and walk him. And spend a little time with him so he won't get too lonesome," Steffie said brightly.

"How long did you say you guys would be gone?"

"Just one day. We're leaving early on Saturday and we'll be back before midnight."

A couple of excursions with Boodles wouldn't kill me. (I told myself Steffie wasn't responsible for the mutt's name, but I knew she probably was.) It would be worth it to score some points with her.

"Please say yes." Steffie said. I'm pretty sure she deliberately used her softest voice.

I had the odd sensation that I had somehow become a powerless spectator, watching from the sidelines as my own life unfolded.

"Sure," I said, "No problem."

Chapter Seventeen

Saturday morning greeted me with an explosion of color in the form of neon sticky notes. It started on the staircase and continued along the hall toward the kitchen.

Every one of them said the same thing. "Boodles."

"The girls were busy before they left," Mom said when I walked into the kitchen.

"Looks like it," I agreed, surveying the bright squares they'd affixed to the counter, cupboards, dishwasher, fridge and various places on the walls.

"I'm surprised you slept through it, the way they were laughing and scurrying about," she added.

I pictured Steffie running around the house, giggling at the thought of my reaction to the Post-it note mayhem. Suddenly I was smiling like a goofball. Which is when I noticed Anna, watching me from the corner of our breakfast nook.

Her eyes were lit up and a creepy smile was spread

across her little mug. I knew immediately that the look on my face had been the last piece of the puzzle for her—she'd finally figured out that it was Steffie I'd been gaga over in the first photobomb.

I poured some cereal into a bowl, sloshed milk over it and slid in across from her. A minute or two later when Mom left the room, Anna pounced, just as I'd known she would.

"So," she said, drawing it out and letting it hang in the air.

I arched an eyebrow and waited.

"I know who you like," she said.

"I like lots of people," I said.

"But you *really* like Steffie."

I looked her right in the eye and smiled. I said nothing.

For the first time ever, Anna seemed just the slightest bit uncertain about what she was about to do. She shook it off and faced me squarely.

"I bet you wouldn't like it if everybody knew," she said. A line I'd heard from her many times before.

I shrugged. I smiled again.

"Who's going to tell them?" I asked.

Anna blinked. Her face grew a frown.

"*I* could," she said.

This was normally the part where she explained what

it would take for her not to divulge whatever bit of information she possessed. Except, she never got a chance — not this time.

"No you won't," I said smoothly. I spooned the last couple of bites of cereal into my mouth and stood up.

"Yes I will!" she insisted.

"I don't think so," I told her. "You've been black-mailing me for years, but that's all over. Because now I know the truth. You're never going to tell."

Anna sputtered a few disconnected sounds. Finally, she got some actual words out.

"I only want three dollars," she said.

"Get it from someone else," I said. "I saw how upset you were when you *accidentally* ratted me out to Mom, remember? You'd never carry out your threats — not on purpose."

I almost felt sorry for her, the way she deflated. She knew she was beat and that there was no going back. I'd just broken free from the family extortionist.

"Now I won't be able to help the animals," Anna said. Tears were welling up in her eyes. Apparently, the sympathy she'd never had for me when she was taking my money was there in full force for creatures she'd never even seen.

"There's still Kim and Paige," I pointed out.

"But you mess up the most," she said sadly. "You were my best customer."

I laughed. "I don't think 'customer' is exactly the right word," I said. "And anyway, there are other ways you can help the animals."

"How?"

"What about volunteering at the shelter?"

I left her thinking about that and headed off to Steffie's house. On the way there I decided my attitude toward Boodles might have been too harsh. After all, the little guy was Steffie's dog. I'd probably been prejudiced by the bad experiences I'd had with Steve's dog Slipper, who will chew up anything he can get his chompers on. And the pack of race-happy, crotch-snorting mutts at the shelter hadn't done anything to change my mind.

By the time I reached the Morton house and pressed in the key code to unlock the door, I was in a more positive frame of mind. Steffie had warned me that Boodles tended to be excited when someone came to the door, so I steeled myself for the yip-yip-yip-yip I knew was coming.

Boodles did not disappoint. He launched into a one-dog yip-fest that continued nonstop as I found his food, opened it, scooped it into his bowl and placed it on the floor in front of him. That doesn't sound as if it should have taken very long, but I didn't see the note telling me where everything was until I'd finished. Too bad Steffie hadn't used a few of those sticky notes to point me toward the dog supplies.

Except for an echo that persisted in my head, the yipping stopped instantly once the food was in front of him. That is *not* to say there was silence while Boodles gobbled his breakfast. You never heard such a racket. That dog was a snorfer and gorber, a chlumper and grucker. He went at his food like he hadn't been fed for weeks, which was clearly not the case considering his midsection was the shape of a drum. I don't know a lot about dog figures, but I kind of doubt "barrel" is the norm.

Little did I suspect the yipping and gorging activities were actually the sanest behavior I was going to see from Boodles. It was as if the food supercharged his crazy batteries. He was probably still swallowing the last bite when he lifted his head, took one quick look at me, and started to leap (as much as a morbidly obese dog *can* leap) and race around.

He dashed between my legs, made a frantic circle of the room and rushed down the hallway as if a pack of dog-catchers was after him. I thought he'd slam into the wall when he got to the end, but he put the brakes on at the last second, turned with the least graceful move an animal could possibly make and raced back. His head was bobbing when he reached me, stopped, looked up for a split second, and set off to repeat the routine.

This went on for a few minutes while I watched, fascinated by the intensity of his performance. There seemed to be real purpose to it, but what the purpose might possibly have been was beyond me. After-feeding exercise maybe. If that was it, he needed to step up the routine.

At last, and as suddenly as it began, it was over. At the end of his final circuit, Boodles shuddered to a halt at my feet and sat there with his tongue lolling halfway to the floor.

"You all right there, buddy?" I asked.

Boodles responded by falling over sideways. For a second I thought he'd had a heart attack from all that running, but then his tail started thumping the floor, so I knew he was still alive. That was a relief. I'd hate to have to tell Steffie her dog keeled over and died the first time he met me.

I reached down, gave his belly a quick rub and asked, "You want to go for a walk?"

Boodles' eyes nearly popped out of their sockets. (Steffie could have warned me that saying "walk" was akin to giving this mutt a giant shot of adrenaline.) He rocketed up and proceeded to bounce up and down like some kind of hound-on-a-spring. Sproing, sproing,

sproing. I swear, a couple of times he shot up so high the two of us were staring straight into each other's eyes. It's anyone's guess whose eyes were wilder just then.

In retrospect, I should probably have found his leash *before* I uttered the magic word. It seemed to take a long, long time to locate it, hanging on a hook inside a hallway closet. Poochie Poo bags hung with it, reminding me that I wasn't only responsible for what went *into* Boodles.

I looked for a plastic scoop like the one I'd been given when I'd walked the shelter dogs, but if the Mortons had one, it was somewhere out of sight.

I'd like to say Boodles settled down and stood calmly waiting to be hooked up once he saw the leash. Except, that would be an enormous lie. When I finally got it connected to his collar, I escorted him out the door and down the street.

Boodles peed (or pretended to) on eleven trees and dumped in a couple of locations on our walk. I tried not to think about what I was picking up when I made use of the Poochie Poo bags, but it was hard to ignore the warmth of the clumps that were separated from my fingers by nothing more than a very thin layer of plastic. While I gathered up the steaming deposits, I looked around carefully, just to be sure no one was watching.

It was a relief to get Boodles back inside and head home.

On the way there, a blast of texts came in from Steffie. I reassured her he'd been fed and walked and promised not to forget to go through the whole wretched business again after supper. Although, that wasn't exactly the way I described it to her.

Her last text wanted to know if I thought he was the sweetest dog ever.

"Unbalanced" was closer to the word I'd have used to describe Boodles. But I didn't tell Steffie that.

Chapter Eighteen

I'd been so focused on the whole business of over-coming my fear of heights that I hadn't paid much attention to the rest of the plan for the skywalking video. It never occurred to me that there could be other things to worry about.

Until Tuesday, when we were at Steve's place eating pizza — one of the frozen kind you cook yourself — and he told me he had someone lined up to shoot the video.

"Yeah? Who?" I asked through the huge bite I'd just taken.

Talking with a mouth full of pizza would have disgusted my sisters. Steve didn't even bat an eye, but before he had a chance to answer my question, there was a knock at his door.

"That should be her now," he said. Then he leaned to one side and hollered down the hall for whoever was there to come on in.

Three seconds later, Riley sauntered into the kitchen.

I stopped chewing.

"Ladies and gentlemen, I give you, our videographer!" Steve announced. Like it was good news.

Riley swept her hand through the air in a half wave. She grinned at me. "Bet *you're* thrilled," she said.

Since my mouth was still full, I just frowned and hoped I was conveying a stony silence.

"Mmm, pizza," Riley said. She grabbed a slice and put it on a paper plate. "I gotta use the bathroom first though — where is it?"

Steve pointed her down the hall. I grabbed a napkin and ejected the pizza I'd been chewing. It had turned into a soggy lump in my mouth.

"Are you crazy?" I whispered furiously. "Why her?"

"She'll be great. She shot some stuff for her old school and it turned out fantastic. Why? What's the problem?"

"She hates me," I said.

"Oh, yeah? What'd you do to her?"

"Nothing," I insisted, annoyed the way he assumed *I* was to blame for any problem there might be between us. "She's got a bad attitude."

That's as far as we got before the bathroom door opened and Riley sailed back into the kitchen, ending our discussion. She picked up her pizza and had it almost to her mouth when her face suddenly contorted into a look of disgust and she put it back down.

"Ew, gross!" she said. I couldn't help noticing she was looking at me.

"No need to be mean," Steve told her. "I admit he's no hunk, but he's not *that* bad."

"What *is* that?" Riley asked, ignoring Steve.

I saw that she was actually looking at the glob of pizza in the napkin I was still holding.

"I saved you a bite," I said, holding it toward her.

Riley made another face, rolled her eyes and turned around so her back was to me. She bit into her slice and made a happy "Mmmm" sound.

"Hey!" I said. "I thought you were vegan. And couldn't eat gluten!"

"Yeah, that got boring."

"You can't just start tolerating gluten because you're bored," I pointed out.

"What are you, my mother?" She plunked onto a chair, still facing away from me.

"I have an idea," Steve said. "How about we drop this and talk about the video?"

I have to admit, Riley had some good ideas, like suggesting we use a fog machine rather than relying on the weather to help mask the Plexiglas cubes. Listening to her describe the shots she was going to get and the music she'd use in the background was enough to distract me from the worry of how I was going to fight off fear and panic. By the time she and Steve had finished planning it all out, I'd even managed to summon some enthusiasm.

The weather forecast suggested that Friday night would be the ideal time. Three days away. I told myself I might as well get it over with instead of having it looming for weeks like a thick, dark cloud. And, at the same time, it gave me a bit of breathing room.

Three days before I had to face my fears.

It was the shortest three days of my life. There hardly seemed to have been enough time to blink before Friday evening was there and the three of us were walking toward the train station.

We made our way along a hard dirt path that skirted the edge of town before it angled downward. It wound its way through a few trees and shrubs until it reached the old abandoned station. The path was too narrow to walk three abreast, but that was fine with me. I hung back a bit behind Steve and Riley, who were yakking away to each other. That gave me a chance to give myself a pep talk.

"I've got this. I can do it," I told myself over and over and over.

Myself didn't believe a word of it.

By the time the train station came into sight my stomach had manufactured what felt like a bubbling pool of molten acid. Even remembering to take slow, deep breaths did little to help. And then, Riley's voice reached me from what seemed a long way away.

"Hey! This place is all boarded up."

My eyes shifted to the structure ahead of us. She was right. Plywood was firmly affixed to every window, and boards had been nailed in place across the huge wooden doors. A couple of faded signs warned against trespassing.

Hope! If we couldn't get *in*, we couldn't get *up*.

But it was a short-lived reprieve.

"Don't worry, I've already been up there," Steve told her cheerfully. "There's a coal door around the side."

Right. I vaguely remembered him telling me that earlier.

"A what?" Riley asked.

"A coal door. The station used coal heat when it was first built, and there was a door for shoveling it into the basement," he explained. "Come on, I'll show you."

We followed him to the back side of the building and found ourselves in front of what looked like an old raft leaning against the wall. It was tilted up at about a twenty-five-degree angle and you could see, through the overgrown grass, that it was resting on some kind of cement base.

"Ladies and gentlemen," Steve said, pointing at it. "Our way in."

He leaned forward and tugged at the side sporting a padlock. It lifted free without objection. A second later the whole door was open. We stood facing a passageway of cement steps.

"What about the no trespassing signs?" I said, even though I knew what Steve's answer would be. I wasn't wrong.

"Those are a hundred years old," he scoffed. "No one pays any attention to this place anymore."

"Okay, so let's go," Riley said. And without another word, she scooted down the damp cement steps and gave the massive door at the bottom a good hard yank. It yielded with a sort of groaning sound, revealing a pitch-black cavern beyond.

I pulled my phone from my pocket and switched on its flashlight, following close behind her. Steve did the same, but even with the two beams of light the darkness was practically suffocating as we moved forward.

Riley said, "Uck," more than once as we made our way through the heavy gloom.

"What is it?" I asked.

"Stupid spiderwebs," she answered.

A moment later we reached a second set of stairs which

let us ascend to the main floor. The light on that level wasn't great either, but it was better than the basement. Slivery beams of sunlight shone in between the wood slats covering the windows. We were in a large open room.

"So, how do we get to the roof from here?" Riley asked.

Steve took us through there and down a hall to an office where a corner door revealed a narrow staircase to the roof. He and Riley scooted up the stairs and I followed — slowly since I was carrying a hundred pounds of dread. On the small landing beside the roof access door I saw the Plexiglas cubes and fog machine, which Steve told us he'd brought earlier.

My stomach clenched as he swung the door open. A burst of light left us squinting while our eyes adjusted.

Steve and Riley stepped forward, away from the doorway, onto the roof. Meanwhile, I noticed my hands were clutching the doorframe, holding on so hard my fingertips were white.

"Come on out," Steve said. "It's really cool — you can see everywhere!"

Those were possibly the least helpful words anyone has ever said to me. Like trying to entice someone to plop their neck down on the guillotine because the blade is nice and sharp.

I tried to remember the strategies I'd planned. Do *not* look down. Concentrate on breathing evenly. Try not to look like a doofus.

I breathed slowly. In through my nose, out through my mouth. I counted each breath. One, two, three, four. Slowly, slowly, I managed to loosen the death grip I had on the doorframe. I kept my eyes focused straight ahead. Steady, steady.

Do not look down.

I took a small step forward. I counted more breaths. Steve and Riley were arranging the Plexiglas cubes. Neither of them seemed to notice my immobility as they got everything set up. When they'd finished, Riley walked around looking for the best angles for our video.

As for me, I was clinging to the words looping around and around in my head. *Do not look down, do not look down, do not look down.*

And then Steve spoke.

"Okay, it's showtime."

CHAPTER NINETEEN

The bones in my legs had turned to rubber. Rubber that was oddly disconnected at the knee. This, as you can imagine, made it difficult to take the few steps I had to conquer in order to reach the waiting Plexiglas cubes.

Steve was already up and walking around on them by the time I'd managed to shuffle my way to the one nearest me.

Meanwhile, Riley had wandered over to the roof's edge — a fact I tried not to register but couldn't quite shut out.

"I *love* this! It's amazing up here," she said. "It feels like you're safe from the whole world."

Safe wasn't the word I'd have picked and I almost heaved when she threw her arms into the air as though she was about to dive off.

I looked away a little too quickly, which caused some sort of tilt inside my head. Slamming my eyes closed, I took a couple of long, deep breaths to steady myself before letting them creep back open.

What a nightmare.

"The fog machine is on so you guys need to be ready as soon as it starts rolling," Riley told us then, her voice suddenly all business. "The batteries won't last long."

"Okay," I croaked.

Steve gave me a curious look.

"You look kind of pale," he said. "Is it that vertigo thing?"

"Yeah," I whispered.

"That's not good," he said. "You want a drink of water or something?"

"I have some water in my pack," Riley said. She'd stopped whatever she'd been doing and was watching me.

My mouth felt like I'd been swallowing fistfuls of dandelion fluff and a few gulps of water would have been great, but all I wanted was to get this whole business over with. Fog had started to seep from the machine. The sooner we got started, the sooner I'd be back on the ground. I waved off the offer, took a deep breath and stepped up onto the nearest cube.

My knees tried to unhinge. That sent a shock of terror through me — a jolt that actually felt as though it had stabbed my heart. Miniature beads of sweat popped out all over my face and neck. In seconds a cold sheen had spread across my forehead and was moving rapidly downward.

It took everything I had to draw a deep breath and steady myself on that cube.

Slow breaths. One. Two. Three. In and out. Eyes locked straight ahead.

I'm not sure how much time passed. Steve was moving around slowly, his hands exploring the air in front of him as though he was finding his way along. I wanted to yell at him to stay away, in case he bumped me. There was no doubt in my mind that the slightest nudge would topple me and that if I began to fall, there would be no end to the plunge.

"Okay, so go ahead and walk around, Derek," Riley said. "Right now it looks like Steve is up here with a statue."

That was when it hit me. In order to take a single step I was going to have to look to see where the other cubes were positioned. Only, the very first downward glance was sure to kick up the panic level that was already threatening to overwhelm me.

I *might* have processed that and figured out a solution, although my brain was moving as sluggishly as I can ever remember, except for what happened next.

A man's voice, deep and gruff, sounded from the ground below.

"Hey! What are you kids doing up there?"

And in spite of the quadrillion times I'd told myself not to do it, my automatic reflexes betrayed me.

I looked down.

There was an instant roar in my ears, like water crashing against rocks. At the same time, my stomach lurched and did a couple of backflips (don't tell me that's impossible, you weren't there). My heart screeched to a complete stop. Luckily, it restarted itself, but then it began to thump with such force I could even feel it in my eyebrows.

Trembling and (I might as well admit it since Riley was recording the whole thing) whimpering, I sank in slow motion, first to my knees and then off the cube and onto the flat surface of the roof. I clawed at the surface, desperate to find something to grasp — but there was nothing to hold onto.

Steve had stopped hopping from cube to cube and was staring at me. Until, that is, Riley took a few steps closer and, with a lowered voice, said the man on the ground had his cell phone out and was calling the police.

"We've gotta get out of here," she said.

Obviously. Or, at least, it was obvious to the two of

them. For me, it was asking the impossible. So, when they started toward the roof entrance back into the building, I stayed right where I was, with my face pressed tight against the gritty surface of the roof.

Steve realized I wasn't with them as they reached the doorway.

"Come on, man," he urged.

I said nothing. But Riley had grasped the truth of the situation.

"He can't move," she said. "He's afraid of heights. We're going to have to leave him."

"We can't do that," Steve said.

Riley sighed and turned to me. "Can you get up and make it over here if we help you?" she asked.

"No," I said. I was one hundred percent immobilized. On the other hand, it felt oddly as though the roof itself was shifting and spinning. As if it was trying to jiggle me to the edge and off.

I squeezed my eyes closed, overcome by terror. Even so, I was aware of Steve and Riley arguing, although I couldn't make out what they were saying over the roar in my head.

In the distance, an abrupt blast of sirens told us the police were close. That seemed to decide the matter for my partners in crime.

"No point in all of us getting busted," Steve called as they began a hasty descent into the building. "But don't worry — they'll help you when they get here."

Riley's voice reached me too, even though she was clearly talking to Steve. "Not if they don't see him, the way he's flattened on the roof."

That comment sent my mind racing from horror to horror although I should have realized Steve would come back to help me if the police didn't find me.

As it happened, the police found me with no trouble. They saw the open cellar door and made their way through the building and up to the roof where the first officer on the scene made what was probably a natural assumption.

"We have a victim of some kind," she called behind her to her partner. "Radio for an ambulance."

She was beside me in a flash and I sensed her kneeling and looking into my face. A couple of fingers pressed against my neck and she exhaled hard in relief when she found a pulse.

"Son? Can you hear me?"

I decided to communicate with moans rather than words. Unfortunately, that only reinforced the officer's idea that I was injured.

The paramedics arrived soon after that and, when they

tried to turn me over, the anguished howl that ripped itself from the pit of my fear froze everyone in place for a few seconds.

But the helpful citizen on the ground was still there, waiting to give his statement on the big crime wave he'd prevented, and he clued in to the scene on the roof.

"I heard one of 'em say the kid who's still up there is scared of heights," he hollered.

"Hoo boy," said the officer who'd reached me first. I didn't think that was very professional of her.

CHAPTER TWENTY

I f I had the power to erase a block of time from my memory, the twenty minutes it took for the emergency workers to get me off the roof would be my first choice. But forgetting is impossible — and not only because it's burned into my brain for all time. My brain is assisted by modern technology.

Apparently, when a siren blares, there are people who will drop everything and race to the scene in the hope that they might witness a complete stranger's misery.

In this case, I was the stranger — a pale and whimpering wretch being pried off a roof, strapped to a stretcher and carried to solid ground by a couple of paramedics. To their credit, they tried hard to calm me, even if their efforts sounded like things you'd say to reassure a two-year-old.

As they reached the ground, a couple of heroic onlookers had the presence of mind to whip out their phones and record that part of my pathetic rescue.

Then the medics took me to the hospital even though I insisted I'd be able to walk as soon as my legs were ready to cooperate again. They loaded my stretcher into the back of the ambulance and the next thing I knew I was in a small examining room in the emergency department.

A nurse took my blood pressure and told me the doctor would be along to examine me shortly. There was a stack of hospital gowns on a counter so I stripped off and got myself ready.

I was sitting on the examining table when my parents arrived. I heard Mom asking someone which room I was in, her voice tight and worried. Then they burst in.

"Are you *hurt*?" Dad asked.

"No, I'm okay."

"What is going on?" Mom said.

"The doctor has to examine me," I said, which coincidentally, was the exact moment he came into the room.

After introducing himself, Doctor Fenton asked me some questions, shone a light in my eyes, told me to stand up and walk to the doorway and back, and said I could go.

Apparently, I'd undressed for nothing.

⌒

BECAUSE BREVAL IS a small place, it took no time for the whole story, along with the videos taken by onlookers, to make its way through the community. It was a safe bet that anyone with a cell phone had seen my sad performance by the end of the day. I could almost hear the message alerts sounding as my escapade raced through town.

The next few days at school were such a misery I actually pitched the idea of home-schooling to my mom, an act of desperation that she shot down with a single question.

"Since your dad and I both work, who exactly is going to home-school you — the goldfish?"

Right.

That was probably for the best anyway. My folks had grounded me indefinitely, making school my only chance to get out of the house.

That didn't mean it was easy. It was no surprise that there was a gigantic decline in my social status. Overnight, I'd become a laughingstock.

(Specifically, a laughingstock who was in trouble with the law, although I didn't know that until later on.)

I held my head up, handled the snickers and comments (which were mostly lame) and tried to act like none of it bothered me. It wouldn't last, I knew that. Those things never do. All I had to do was let it roll off me until everyone got bored saying the same things over and over.

Not that they were all *exactly* the same. One girl shoved her impudent face at me and told me to lose her number. That was puzzling since I had no idea who she was and I'd *definitely* never called her. Maybe she'd slipped it to me back when I was riding high on the fickle wave of approval.

For the record, a few kids tried to be helpful. They told me not to let it get to me and things like that. I appreciated it, even though most of them whispered their words of encouragement like undercover spies when no one else was around.

The one exception was Denise, who grinned and gave me a cheery wave as she met me on my way to gym class on Tuesday.

"Skylah says hi," she said, good and loud. "And she said not to worry about what just happened because only *cats* are perfect."

"Tell her thanks!" I said, surprised at how much a few friendly words had cheered me up.

Moments later, a new worry came at me. I was getting my gym shoes on when my name came over the PA system. I was being called down to the office. On the way there I had time to wonder how the growing fiasco of my life might have landed me in trouble at school.

I scuffed my way there as slowly as possible. The

secretary, Mrs. Floutworthy, gave me a disapproving look, but since gloom and disappointment are her go-to expressions, I tried not to worry. She shook her head sadly, as if she couldn't quite believe what a disappointment I was to the world in general.

"You called for me?" I said when I'd stood there for at least ten seconds and she still hadn't spoken.

"Principal wants you," she told me with a mournful sigh. "Just go right in."

The door was open to Ms. Lam's office, but I stopped and waited for her to signal me in.

"Oh, Derek," she said when she noticed me. "Come in and have a seat."

"Did I do something wrong?" I asked as I lowered myself into one of two identical black cloth chairs that faced her desk.

"Wrong?" she said. "No. Nothing like that. But your teachers and I are concerned with things happening in your life — outside of school."

My brain was still in trouble mode, so I braced myself to hear what kind of problems the roof incident was going to cause next.

"I wanted to offer you a chance to talk to someone — if you'd like to," she continued.

"Who?" I asked.

"A counselor," she said. "Someone who can help you navigate through some of the challenges you may be facing."

I thought about that for a moment.

"No thanks," I said at last. "I mean, I appreciate the offer and everything, but I think I'm okay."

"That's fine," she said. "But if anything changes or you find you're struggling dealing with this, don't be afraid to let me, or any of your teachers, know. We're here to give you whatever support we can."

"Okay, thanks," I said.

Ms. Lam smiled, stood, and shook my hand before I left.

My steps seemed lighter walking back to class. It felt good to know the school had my back! Funny how I'd assumed the worst — and I wasn't the only one. Walking home at the day's end, Steve asked me if I was in trouble.

"Because I got called to the office?" I said. "No, Ms. Lam was just checking if I was okay."

"About what?"

"What do you mean about what?" I said. "Everyone in town knows about Friday night."

"Oh," Steve said. He looked at his feet. "I still feel terrible about taking off and abandoning you like that."

"Forget it," I said.

"It's just that I *panicked*," he said, like that might be news to me.

I got why he'd left me stranded. And I knew he probably couldn't have done anything to help. It would just have meant trouble for him too.

I told him that, but he still felt bad, judging by how many times he said he'd make it up to me. But *then* he said something that made my hair stand on end.

"I'll try to persuade Riley to get rid of the video she took on the roof," he said. "It's kind of too bad, though. Now no one will ever see me skywalking."

I'd somehow forgotten that the videos taken on the ground were by no means the worst ones that were shot that day. And who knew how much worse the one Riley had taken on the roof was?

As it turned out, Steve did. He had the video on his phone. He admitted Riley had sent it to him the same day we'd been up there.

I didn't *want* to see it, but it was one of those situations where I couldn't help myself. I told him to forward it, which he did.

I braced myself and tapped *Play*.

It was worse than I could ever have imagined. SO much worse, although it started out kind of cool. There was Steve, moving through the mist, doing his skywalking stunt. It was perfect — a hauntingly cool sight.

And then it moved to me.

I wonder how many people have ever seen that much fear on a human face. Terror spilled from me in waves as clearly as the fog that rolled and drifted in the space between the roof and my feet.

If anyone in town doubted I was the biggest coward on the planet after seeing the other videos, they'd be dead certain of it if they ever saw this one.

I watched it through to the end, all two minutes forty-one seconds, and then forced myself to start over. It somehow seemed even worse the second time. I stopped halfway through.

There was no denying it. Riley's video was a hundred times more humiliating than the ones that had already been shared. Cold sweat prickled the back of my neck. I could practically hear the roars of laughter.

Steve seemed to think he could talk her into deleting it, but I wasn't counting on that happening. If there was one thing I knew for sure about Riley, it was that she did not like me. At all.

Fate had definitely turned on me. And it wasn't through yet.

CHAPTER TWENTY-ONE

My steps slowed to a near halt as I rounded the corner to my street and saw the police car sitting in our driveway. I didn't know *what* they wanted, but it wasn't hard to figure out *who* they were there to see.

The cruiser wasn't the only thing that seemed out of place. There was also Paige, out on the front step, peering from side to side with her hand shielding her eyes from the sun, like a lookout on the bowsprit of a pirate ship.

Until she spied me. The second she did, a look of great joy lit up her face and she came pelting down the sidewalk. She was moving at such rocket speed that she barely got stopped in time to avoid crashing into me.

"You're in trouble with the police," she said with absolutely no attempt to disguise the happiness this was bringing her.

I sidestepped my gloating sister and picked up my pace, partly to get away from her and partly to get off the street and away from any lurking cameras. I had no particular reason to think anyone was capturing what was happening, but I'd learned it was *always* possible someone might be.

In spite of my increased speed, Paige shifted into high gear and zipped past me as I reached the door.

"I found him!" she announced importantly, as if she had single-handedly ended a nation-wide manhunt.

I stepped inside where I found a couple of officers waiting in the living room. Next to them were Anna, Kim, and ... *Steffie*. Terrific.

They introduced themselves as Officers Jankowski and Donegan. Jankowski was tall and thin. He gave me a friendly smile which made it hard to imagine him getting tough on crime. Not that there's much of that around here.

Donegan was the officer who thought she'd found a corpse, or at the very least a stabbing victim, when she'd first seen me on the roof of the train station. I drew myself up to my full five-foot-four-inch height and squared my shoulders, hoping for a manlier impression than I'd made on our first encounter.

"How are you, Derek?" she asked.

"I'm good," I said, lowering my voice so I'd sound stronger and braver than the version of me she'd seen before. That was a mistake, judging by the strange, deep sound that came out of my mouth.

Paige snorted out a laugh and said, "What are you supposed to be, a robot?"

Officer Donegan ignored her. "We're just waiting for one of your parents to get here, Derek," she said.

"I called Mom," Kim said helpfully.

Even though my head was spinning with questions about what the police wanted, I still managed to be aware of Steffie's eyes on me. She wasn't the only one who was practically staring, but she was the only one whose opinion I cared about.

Officer Jankowski made some small talk while we waited, breaking off in mid-sentence when we heard footsteps hurrying up the walk.

"I got here as fast as I could," Mom said, flinging the door open and stepping inside. Her eyes darted around taking in the cluster of people gathered in the room. She quickly took command of the situation.

"Girls, upstairs. All of you." She turned then to the officers, extending a hand and saying, "I'm Ali Cowell, Derek's mom."

The girls dragged their feet, but even so, the only thing they could have heard would have been the police introducing themselves to Mom, and Mom offering them coffee, which was politely refused.

"Then I guess you can go ahead and tell us what this is about," Mom said.

"We're following up on the incident this past Friday," said Officer Donegan.

"The one where Derek was assisted off the roof of the old train station," Officer Jankowski added, as if there'd been a bunch of incidents and he wanted to be sure we knew which one they were talking about.

"We have a few questions for Derek," Donegan said.

"Is Derek in trouble?" Mom asked.

"Derek was trespassing," Donegan said. She spoke slowly, as though she was choosing her words carefully. "And as a result of that action, emergency services had to be called."

"Will there be charges?" Mom said.

"Well, that may depend," Officer Jankowski said. "We understand there were two or three others up there, but they fled before we arrived on the scene."

My throat was instantly dry.

"We can go easier on Derek if he cooperates and gives us the names of his accomplices," Donegan said.

"Accomplices," Mom repeated faintly. She looked at me. "How many of you were up there?"

I gave her a pleading look. I shook my head slightly, to show her I couldn't — wouldn't — rat anyone out.

Mom turned back to face the officers.

"Are you talking about criminal charges?" she said.

"He can probably avoid that *if* he cooperates," said Donegan.

"But the others would be charged in that case?" Mom asked.

"Possibly, but Derek would be dealt with by the Diversion Program," Jankowski said.

Donegan added, "Don't forget, they left him up there to take the rap by himself."

A horrible feeling of dread settled in my chest. Mom *had* to know Steve was involved. What if she decided to give him up to make things easier for me?

There was silence for a long moment or two. I stared at the floor, hardly breathing. And then Mom stood up.

"I think perhaps I should speak with an attorney before we go any further with this conversation," she said.

Officer Jankowski scowled as he and Donegan got to their feet. "The offer of leniency could be withdrawn at any time," he said.

"Noted," Mom said coldly. But her face softened as she escorted them to the door and before they left she thanked them for helping me when I needed it.

I waited, expecting a lecture or interrogation or something. Instead, Mom walked past me without a glance.

She went straight to the phone and made a call. To her attorney, apparently, though I was surprised she actually had one. I always thought the only people who needed lawyers were criminals.

The amazing thing was, later on, after Mom and Dad had talked it over, they both agreed it would be wrong for me to turn in anyone else in order to save myself.

"Our lawyer will speak to the prosecutor and make the best arrangement he can," Mom explained.

I spent a lot of time wondering about this arrangement. It was hard not to picture myself being locked up in some kind of juvenile jail, surrounded by gang members who spent all their spare time working out and thinking up ways to torture scrawny guys like me. I wondered if I should start honing my begging-for-mercy skills. Or maybe I had time to get a macho tattoo before I got sent to the slammer. (Like Mom would let me.)

After enduring the snide remarks at school for the past few days I'd convinced myself the worst was behind me. Now, the law was after me and I had no idea what was going to come of that. It seemed that, after all, the worst was still to come.

And, it turned out, I didn't know the half of it.

Chapter Twenty-Two

Anna never does anything I tell her to do. Normally, she actually does the exact opposite. And she loves to tell me I am *not* the boss of her, or, in fact, the boss of anyone or anything.

So it was a bit of a surprise this Saturday, when she took my advice and went to volunteer at the animal shelter. She even asked me a few questions before heading out. I was tempted to prank her — just a little — by giving her a bogus list of things to take along, but something about her face made me change my mind. I wished her good luck instead.

She was gone for most of the afternoon, and when she came home it was with shining eyes, an announcement that Denise is the nicest person she ever met, and a cage with a seriously overweight rabbit.

"Mom will never let you keep that," Paige said. Paige had been extra grumpy since early this morning when Kim, the WORST sister ever, tried to ruin her life. I didn't get all the details, but it had something to do with the PVR and some reality show.

"I'm just babysitting him for a while, and Mom already said I *could*," Anna answered. "Plus, bunny doesn't have a name so I get to call him whatever I want."

Paige shrugged and went to find other opportunities for spreading misery.

"I'm going to call him Nibbles," Anna said, kneeling down in front of the cage and peering in. "Do you think he'd like that?"

"I don't think rabbits care what you call them," I said. "And don't get too attached. You know you can't keep him."

"Mom said I can keep him for two weeks if I take care of him," she said huffily.

But on Sunday morning it seemed doubtful Nibbles would be with us anywhere near that long.

I woke up early, peed and headed downstairs for a glass of apple juice before going back to bed. That's when I discovered the bountiful bunny had somehow managed to get out of the cage during the night.

I hadn't even made it to the bottom of the stairs when I saw the first batch of rabbit deposits. (I don't have to spell that out, right?) I paused on the bottom step, peering as far as I could see in all directions. Nibbles had been hard at work — all night long by the look of it.

I picked my way cautiously down the hall toward the kitchen, which is where I found him, sitting on the mat in front of the sink. My guess would be that he needed rest. Covering that many floors with turds must have taken a lot out of him. (Good one, huh?)

"You'll be gone before noon, pal," I told him. He twitched his nose.

There wasn't the slightest doubt in my mind that I was right. Mom would freak when she saw what he'd done. I could practically hear the screeches.

Anna now had about as much chance of keeping that rabbit for two weeks as I had of being Steffie's date for the prom. Not that I'd ever imagined what that would be like. Not seriously anyway.

Anna's not much for hiding her feelings, so I knew we'd all be listening to her boo-hooing once Nibbles got sent packing. I could almost see her, going around with a droopy face and trembling lip, but that wouldn't be the worst of it. Anna can manufacture the most horrible, shuddering sobs you ever heard when she's heartbroken about something.

Aw, heck.

I grabbed the dumb rabbit so I could jam him back into his cage. He put up a fight, kicking and struggling, and, at one point, catching my nose with a flailing foot. I finally stuffed him in, slammed the door shut, and made sure it was solidly latched. My nose was bleeding slightly from his claw or hoof or whatever a rabbit has, but it was just a drop or two. Nothing I couldn't wipe off on my sleeve.

It didn't take as long as I'd expected to sweep up the scattered balls of bunny poop. Thankfully, they're hard and dry, unlike the puddles I found in the laundry room off the kitchen. I swabbed those up with the mop and squirted the floor with some kind of spray.

Then I went back to bed. The second time I went downstairs, a couple of hours later, Anna and Dad were outside and the rabbit was with them. Dad was making some kind of temporary shelter for it in the backyard.

I slid the kitchen window open and said, "What's up?"

Anna swung around and, seeing me there, stuck her tongue out and told me it was none of my business.

I was annoyed for a couple of seconds, but I reminded myself she didn't know what I'd done for her earlier. Besides, she was probably still upset over losing her best blackmail *customer*. That thought actually made me smile.

"What happened to your nose?"

I jumped a bit. Mom had come up behind me and was

looking at the scratch mark handsomely displayed in the middle of my face.

"Nothing. The rabbit clawed me."

The way she reacted, you'd have thought I'd said I'd been in the festering jaws of a Komodo dragon.

"You were clawed by a *wild animal*?" she said.

"I think it's tame if it lives in a cage," I said. I thought that was a valid point, but Mom didn't seem to agree.

"The shelter won't be open today," she said, moving toward the phone. "Do you have the number for the woman who runs it?"

"No," I said. "And why do you want to call her anyway?"

"To find out if the rabbit has been vaccinated for rabies," Mom said.

"Denise might have the number," I said. I have no idea what prompted me to say this. Maybe Mom's agitated state activated some kind of self-destruct auto-pilot in my brain.

"Well call and ask her!"

"I'll send her a text," I said.

"*Calling* is faster," Mom insisted. Her face told me there would be no arguing.

I scrolled through my contacts, found Denise, and hit dial. She answered on the fourth ring.

"Hey. Do you have Gabby's number?" I said.

The worried-mother expression hovering in front of me changed instantly to horrified.

"Is *that* the way you start a conversation?" Mom hissed.

"Uh, sorry," I blurted, cutting off whatever Denise was trying to say. "I mean, Hello. This is Derek."

Silence for a second. A snicker and then, "Hello, Derek. This is Denise."

I repeated the request for Gabby's number. I remembered to say please.

So, of course she wanted to know why I needed it.

"My mom wants it," I mumbled.

"Oh, yeah?" She hesitated. "Is it important? Because I don't know if I'm supposed to give it out."

"Uh, kind of, I guess." I glanced at Mom, whose eyes were boring into me. "I got attacked by um, a wild animal."

"Why would your mom be calling Gabby for *that*?"

"It was a shelter animal," I admitted slowly.

There was a silent pause. I could tell she was waiting for more, or trying to sort out what I was saying in a way that made sense. Then she put it together.

"You mean the *rabbit* your sister took home?" she asked.

"Something like that," I said, because being vague was

almost definitely going to throw her off track.

It took a minute for Denise to stop laughing long enough to give me the number.

But when Mom dialed Gabby's place (yes, to complain that a big vicious rabbit brutalized her precious baby) there was no answer.

I foolishly thought that might be the end of it, but Mom had a new plan.

"I think we should have you checked just in case."

"What do you mean, have me checked?"

"At the hospital."

My mom isn't much of a jokester, so I knew she wasn't kidding around, even though it was hard to believe she was about to haul me to a doctor over a scratch.

When we got to the emergency department, the nurse who registered me seemed to have a hard time grasping what I was doing there. (He wasn't the only one.) I'm nearly positive he was holding back a smirk when he put the paper bracelet on my wrist and told us to have a seat and a doctor would see me shortly.

Two hours later I was called into an examining room and moments after that the doctor on call walked in. My heart sank to see that it was Dr. Fenton, the same one who'd tended to me after the train station roof. Just my luck.

Then again, I thought, he probably wouldn't even remember me. There must be hundreds of patients through outpatients every week.

Dr. Fenton looked at the chart, read, "Wild animal abrasion," out loud, and then turned toward me. His eyes widened.

"You can keep your clothes on," he said quickly. "Now, let's have a look at the injury."

"It's this claw-mark," Mom said, pointing. "On his nose."

Dr. Fenton leaned forward for a closer look at my dangerous wound.

"And this scratch was from..." he paused to consult the chart again. "What kind of animal?"

"A rabbit," Mom said. "It doesn't look like much, but we were concerned about the possibility of rabies."

"*I* wasn't," I said.

Dr. Fenton smiled. "You were right to have it checked out," he told Mom. He asked about the rabbit and when Mom told him it was from the shelter he said we should keep an eye on it for the next couple of weeks.

"Rabies is more commonly transmitted through saliva, and rabbits aren't typical carriers," he said. "*But* if this rabbit should become ill, or display any unusual behaviors, bring Derek in again and we'll re-evaluate."

I was back at home, recovering from the embarrassment of being taken to Emergency for a scratch you could barely see, when a message pinged on my phone from Denise.

Are you going to pull through?
I'm worried sick over here!

I couldn't help laughing.

Looks like I'll make it,
but my nose might have
to come off.

A couple of minutes passed before she answered that.

Tough break. But at least there's
a bright side.

Yeah? What's that?

The rabbit's okay.

I smiled. That rabbit had all the luck. He'd gotten away with pooping all over the house and then attacking the person who saved him from eviction. His punishment had been to have a shelter and penned-in area built so he could run around and enjoy himself in the backyard.

Meanwhile, I was practically a social pariah at that

point. But after seeing things change overnight more than once I knew another turnaround was possible.

All I needed was a lucky break.

Chapter Twenty-Three

Tuesday afternoon I got called to the office at school. Again.

It had *not* been what you could call a good day up until then. The snickers and eye-rolling just kept coming and there'd been plenty of half-heard comments — the kind where I'd catch my name and a word or two. Enough that I could tell they weren't whispering compliments.

Mrs. Floutworthy was sorting papers in front of a filing cabinet when I walked into the office and crossed over to the counter. She didn't even glance up, though I knew she was aware I was there.

"AHEM!" I said. Loudly.

Mrs. Floutworthy darted a glance behind me and lifted her hands up like she had no idea what to make of this nasty kid in front of her.

I turned uneasily. And there was my mother, getting up from one of the visitors' chairs along the back wall.

"Mom!" I said. "I didn't know you were coming here."

"Obviously," Mom said. She nodded toward Mrs. Floutworthy. "I believe you have something you'd like to say to the school secretary."

"Office Administrator," Mrs. Floutworthy corrected, drawing herself up to her full height, which is about five foot two.

"Of course. I beg your pardon," Mom said. "Derek?"

"Sorry," I mumbled.

Mrs. Floutworthy pressed her lips tight and gave me a stiff nod. She turned to Mom.

"I imagine you've got your hands full with that one," she said.

That was a mistake. Mom will correct our behavior when she thinks one of us is out of line, but there was no way she'd ever put up with a stranger badmouthing a kid of hers.

"Actually," she said coldly. "Derek is a fine young man who, like the rest of us, sometimes makes mistakes."

That made me feel good — until we got to the car. That's when Mom filled me in on why she'd pulled me out of class.

"We have a meeting with a worker from the Diversion Program," she said. She explained that our lawyer had made a deal to settle the trespassing thing.

"I thought I could only get that program if I ratted out Ste … the others who were there," I said.

"Yes. Well, apparently the prosecutor felt differently."

Relief washed over me. I didn't have to worry about being sent to a detention center full of giant goons after all.

"That's great," I said.

"You were lucky — this time," Mom said. "And I'm not going to lecture you because I know you've already had a lot of embarrassment over the incident, but you need to think things through more. You're a smart kid. Your father and I expect you to act like it."

I hung my head. "Sorry," I said. My second apology in less than half an hour, but this time I meant it.

Mom reached over and patted my arm, which somehow made me feel horrible. I noticed that she looked tired and sort of sad and I knew I was to blame. She probably never expected she'd be dealing with problems with the law for one of her kids.

The building she pulled up to was also tired and sad looking — built of chunky brown stones and cement steps that widened at the bottom like a frowning mouth. I trudged up them behind Mom and followed her down a gloomy hallway to a large wooden door with a frosted window in the top. A sign on the door said "Probation

Services: Diversion and Public Education."

Inside, we found ourselves facing an empty desk, but there were two rooms that branched off the reception area and from one of these a woman's voice told us to take a seat and said she'd be right with us.

We sat obediently and a few moments later the clickety-click-click of heels tapped their way across the room to us. The woman balanced on the heels had a mean glint in her eyes that put me on instant alert.

"I'm Sabrina Lake," she said nodding quickly to Mom and then to me. "Please come with me."

In less than five minutes my first impression was confirmed. Ms. Lake (as she told me to call her) was hard and tough and wanted to make sure I knew it.

"You're on the wrong path, Derek," she said, squaring her shoulders and frowning. "My job is to *try* to steer you onto the right one before it's too late. If you don't make changes — big changes — and make them *now*, you're going right, straight down the toilet."

I thought Mom might speak up like she had with Mrs. Floutworthy, but she never said a word. In fact, she even nodded a couple of times, as if she totally agreed that I was on the verge of a life of crime.

"Anyway," Ms. Lake said after she'd finished with the dire predictions. "The first step toward rehabilitation is learning responsibility. In your case, that will start with community service."

On the way there, Mom had explained that part of doing this program meant I would be given 80 hours of whatever unpaid work they found for me. (This used to be called slave labor, but I decided not to mention that.) I was curious to know what I'd be doing so I paid close attention as Ms. Lake pulled some papers out of a file folder that topped a stack on her desk and slid them toward me.

"I've found you a placement," she tapped the top page. "You'll be helping with a restoration project at the rec center every Saturday."

"What do I have to do?" I asked.

"Whatever they ask you to do — you have no skills so it will be menial — carrying supplies, cleaning, that sort of thing."

She went over a few more details of the community service, got me to sign some forms and then gave me the name and number of the person who'd be supervising me. Serge Durand. I was to call him to get my schedule.

"Mr. Durand will be reporting back to me on your performance," she said pointedly. Then she added, "I expect to hear nothing but good things." Her tone suggested she actually expected the exact opposite.

When we got back home Mom said I should call Mr. Durand right away, so he'd know I was eager to get started. That wasn't the word I'd have used to describe how I felt about 80 hours of unpaid labor, but I dutifully went to the phone and made the call.

Mr. Durand told me to be at the rec center on Saturday morning at seven.

"Seven o'clock in the *morning*?" I said, sure I'd heard him wrong.

"I get there at five," he said. "So you can come earlier if you want. But the other kid in the program starts at seven."

Then he hung up.

CHAPTER TWENTY-FOUR

"So, are you still grounded now that your lawyer got everything taken care of?"

Good old Steve. He didn't waste any time sympathizing over the 80 hours I'd be slaving away at the rec center, or the crazy time of morning I was going to have to drag myself there. Nope. He got straight to the part that affected him. Or, as he'd mentioned a few times already, *he* was bored when I couldn't hang out.

I wasn't feeling a whole lot of sympathy for his misfortune.

"Dad says he and Mom will talk it over and let me know this weekend," I said.

"At least if they let me come over we could find something to do at your place," he said, then added nervously, "But do they know I was involved? I mean, did they ask you?"

"Seriously? You think they needed to ask?" I said. "Because they'd never have figured that out on their own?"

Steve offered me a weak grin, said, "Yeah, I guess you're right," and promptly dropped it.

That was the end of him complaining about not being allowed over when I was grounded. No one would ever accuse Steve of being overly sensitive, but even he probably wasn't eager to face my folks when they knew he'd gotten off scot-free for stuff I was in a bunch of trouble over. Especially when the whole thing had been his idea.

On Friday I made a suggestion.

"Hey, I know a way we can hang out for a while. You could give me a hand at the rec center tomorrow. As a volunteer."

He gawked at me open-mouthed for so long I started to think his jaw had come unhinged. As soon as he regained control, he stammered out a question.

"Don't you think that would make me look guilty?"

"You *are* guilty," I pointed out.

His eyes narrowed. Red patches blotched his neck and chased each other all the way up to his hairline. It almost amused me, how the conversation was doing such interesting things with his face.

"Yeah, but—" he said. Not much of an argument, and yet apparently all he had just then.

"I'm messing with you," I said, which he immediately claimed he'd known the whole time.

And of course, I went to the rec center by myself on Saturday morning. I'd mostly been joking when I'd suggested Steve should come along, but as I trudged sleepily toward the hulking building, I couldn't help thinking it would have been nice to have a friend with me.

It was just past seven when I pushed open the wide double doors that led into the entrance area. I hoped Durand wasn't too much of a stickler. I sure didn't want him telling Ms. Lake that I'd been late the very first day, even if it was only a few minutes.

He was nowhere in sight, but I could hear voices coming from the auditorium so I made my way there and stuck my head in.

The first person I saw had to be Mr. Durand. He wasn't a whole lot taller than me, but thick-chested and swarthy with a few days' growth of chin stubble. His hair was thick and dark and didn't appear to have met up with a comb that morning. He didn't look much like the manager of a town building.

As soon as he noticed me he gestured for me to come in. I'd taken a couple of steps when my brain registered who the person standing next to him was.

Riley!

"What are you doing here?" I blurted.

"Same as you," said the man. "She's here to work. Assuming you're Derek Cowell."

I told him I was.

"I'm Serge Durand," he grunted. "You can call me Serge."

Serge bent to pick up a clipboard, which was laying on top of a box of assorted cleaning supplies. As he scanned whatever was written there, I turned to Riley.

"How did *you* get caught?"

She gave me a deadly glare. The kind that means I'll pulverize you if you say another word. I stopped talking.

Serge glanced up from his clipboard and looked back and forth between us. "What's that?" he said.

"Who knows?" Riley shrugged. "He's a weirdo."

Serge cleared his throat.

"I'm not here to babysit, so whatever your personal history is, you'd better be able to work together."

"Yes, sir," Riley said quickly.

"No problem," I agreed.

"Good," he said. "So, I'll go over what I want you to do today."

Our first job was to clean the thick wooden baseboards in the gym so they could be repainted. We each got buckets along with scouring pads and sponges for scrubbing.

I started on the left side and Riley took the right. As soon as we were alone, I asked her again how she got caught.

"You really aren't very smart are you?" she said. "If I was here for *that*, why would I care if you asked about it in front of Serge?"

Slowly, like a fluorescent bulb, flickering and fizzing at first, the light came on.

"You mean you're in trouble for something else?" I asked.

"Yeah, genius," she snapped. "So keep your mouth shut about the roof business."

"I'm no rat," I said. "So, what are you here for?"

As soon as I'd asked, I knew it was a dumb question. Riley didn't bother answering. She rolled her eyes and shook her head without even glancing in my direction.

That summed up our conversation for the next few hours. I got to work, scrubbing and scraping — you wouldn't believe the amount of crud that was built up on those baseboards. I was still about ten feet from the first corner by the middle of the morning.

That's when Riley lowered her standards and spoke to me again, but it was only because she wanted to switch places.

"You haven't even finished half as much as me," I

pointed out. I didn't bother mentioning the reason for that, which was the amount of time she was spending texting and messing around on her phone instead of working.

"Just for a little while — then we'll trade back," she said. "There's some tough stuff here that needs more muscle than I have."

I'm not stupid. I knew she was trying to flatter me so I'd do what she wanted, but I decided it might be worth the effort. Maybe if I did something nice for her, she'd act a little more civil. I hadn't asked her how many hours of community service she was stuck with, but however long we were going to be working together, it was bound to go easier if she was less hostile.

So we switched places. I knelt down, looking for whatever she'd found hard to clean. It all looked pretty much the same as the other side. I shrugged and started cleaning.

And then the door opened and Serge came in.

"Break time," he said. "You have fifteen minutes."

Riley stood up from where she'd been scrubbing vigorously when Serge arrived. She wiped the back of her hand across her forehead.

"Wow," she said. "Is it ten o'clock already?"

Serge gave her a quick nod, but it was me he was

mainly looking at. I could see him comparing the prog-ress it seemed I'd made with the area Riley had apparently covered.

He did not look impressed.

"Maybe pick up the pace a bit, Derek," he said while Riley gave me a huge smile in the background.

"Yes, sir," I said.

And I did. She might have got me then, but for the rest of the day I worked like a madman, scrubbing and scraping like my life depended on it. Even though she kept working on the left I was soon ahead of her on the right side.

That forced her to work harder to try to keep up, but I was still a good fifteen feet out front by the end of the day. My arms were aching as we carried our buckets and cleaning supplies to the office where Serge had to fill our shifts in on some forms and get us to sign them.

Riley's aunt was waiting for her near the entrance as we passed by, a detail I registered without interest.

But then Serge said something that grabbed my attention.

"I'll get your paperwork done first, Riley, since your foster mom is waiting for you."

CHAPTER TWENTY-FIVE

Riley's face flushed and she darted a glance at me, looking to see if I'd registered what Serge had just said.

I had.

Even so, she did her best to act nonchalant as she signed the form and slunk out of the office. I wasn't buying it.

She *had* to be worried. After all, I'd just discovered that what she'd told everyone about herself was a lie. She wasn't staying with relatives, and her parents for darn sure weren't working for Doctors Without Borders.

I wondered what the truth might be. Why would she make all that stuff up? I could see why she might want to keep her status as a foster kid private. It was nobody's business if her family was having problems that needed that kind of support.

But if she was in care because of whatever she'd done to get community service, *that* was different.

It was doubtful anyone else knew she wasn't who she'd

been claiming to be. Well, except for her fake "cousin" Trisha. But Trisha hadn't told anyone. If she had, it would have gotten around. Maybe Riley had intimidated her into keeping quiet. It wasn't hard to picture that happening.

But now *I* knew.

Here she'd been acting like she was so much better than everyone else when the whole time all her bragging had been nothing but lies. Which made her a liar and a lawbreaker.

And sure, I'm doing community service over my own trouble with the law. But it's hard to see myself as some kind of renegade outlaw for being on a roof.

Anyway, it didn't really matter what *she'd* done to get herself community service. It was enough knowing she'd lied about who she was.

For the record, I had no actual plan to expose her. That would have made me a complete jerk.

But she didn't know that, which had to have her worried. That made me feel sorry for her for about two seconds. And then it passed.

The walk home was suddenly a pleasant thing. The sky was bluer, the sun was brighter, the air felt light and clean.

Until I remembered something, and a dark cloud descended.

I was *supposed* to go straight home, but I changed direction without even thinking about it. A quick stop at Steve's place had to be worth the small risk of getting caught.

He was sprawled on the couch watching music videos and spooning globs of ice cream into his mouth straight out of the container — something that would be a capital offense in my house.

"Hey!" He sat forward with the groan of someone who'd overestimated how much ice cream his stomach could handle. "You finally allowed out in the real world again?"

"I don't know yet, and anyway that's not why I'm here."

Steve muted the sound on the TV and looked at me expectantly.

"That video Riley shot on the roof of the train station—"

"What about it?" he asked.

"Did she *really* erase it off her phone?"

"She said she did."

"But do you know *for sure*?"

Steve squinted at me, like I was out of focus. "How could I know for sure?"

"Like, did you *see* her erase it?"

He hadn't, of course. All he could tell me was what

she'd told him. And if I'd just learned anything about Riley it was that she was *not* one hundred percent committed to the truth.

Back on the street and headed for home I decided she'd think twice about sharing the video even if she did still have it. Not when I had information about her she wouldn't want getting around. It was sort of a stalemate.

These thoughts were interrupted by the familiar sight of my mom's car, turning at the corner up ahead. I almost lifted an arm to wave her over for a ride, which would have been an incredibly dumb mistake. Not because my mom wouldn't pick me up, but because she'd know by the street I was on that I was coming from Steve's, not the rec center. It would have destroyed any chance that my grounding would end anytime soon.

Panic rushed over me as the car swung in my direction and started down the street. If Mom hadn't already seen me, she would in a matter of seconds.

I hurled myself on the ground between a couple of bushes and crawled snake-style through onto the nearest yard. Then I turned and watched between the lower branches to see if Mom slowed down or pulled over.

The car crept into view and rolled right on by. I caught a glimpse of Mom, facing forward with no sign that she'd spotted me.

I relaxed, realized I'd been holding my breath, and exhaled in a huff of relief. I figured I'd give Mom a couple of minutes to be well out of sight and then I'd be on my way.

That's when I became aware of footsteps approaching from the direction of the house. I turned slowly, expecting to find myself looking up at a curious, or possibly angry, homeowner.

Instead, I found Denise bent over and staring into my face!

"Is this your place?" I blurted.

"Mmm hmm. But most of our visitors just use the front walk," she said, grinning.

I scrambled to my feet. "You're probably wondering what I'm doing," I said.

She straightened up so we were face to face and smiled wider.

"The question crossed my mind," she agreed.

I wasn't about to tell her the exact truth — that I was a loser hiding from his mommy. But for some reason, I didn't want to tell her a complete lie either. So I compromised.

"The thing is, I'm a criminal on the lam," I whispered, leaning in. "There's a posse out, hunting me down like a dog, and I needed somewhere to hide."

Denise laughed. And she leaned in too, and whispered

back, "You can hide out here — *unless* — do you happen to know if there's a reward for turning you in?"

That made me laugh too. But once we both stopped laughing something weird happened. We stood there, not moving, just looking at each other.

Our faces were close. Really close. And the next thing I knew, our mouths were touching and my heart was banging and thumping so hard I bet she heard it.

I don't know much (anything, actually) about kisses. It felt like it was over awfully quick, but I had no idea how long it was supposed to last. When we moved apart Denise smiled again — but it was a different kind of smile than I'd seen from her before. It was like she was happy and scared at the same time. Like she was confused.

She wasn't the only one. My whole brain was short-circuiting, which is the only way I can explain my next genius move.

I blurted, "Okay, so I gotta go!"

Then I shoved my way through the bushes back to the sidewalk and took off for home.

CHAPTER TWENTY-SIX

Fortunately, I didn't bump into anyone I knew on the rest of the walk home. It's impossible to say what kind of babble might have come out of me if I'd been required to speak just then.

I, Derek Cowell, had kissed a girl!

Or, had *she* kissed *me*? Maybe we'd kissed each other. I had no clue and didn't much care. What mattered was that it had been the real thing, not something that happened because of some silly challenge. It was a regular kiss — with someone I liked.

Which was another surprise. I'd never thought of Denise quite that way before. Except, as soon as that thought came to me, I knew it wasn't true.

Somewhere along the way I'd started to like Denise. I mean, I liked her as a friend almost right away, but it had turned into a different kind of like. I just hadn't put it all together until now.

I wondered if it was the same for her.

And now one or both of us had made a move — I seriously had no idea how I was ever going to figure out if it had been me or her. It's not like I could ask. And maybe she didn't know either.

Whatever. Not only had we kissed, but it had been nice. Really nice. Better than nice.

It had been *great*.

As I crossed the lawn toward to my front door I pictured Denise's face and the sort of trembling smile she'd given me right afterward. She was so cute!

I smiled like a goof. Hopefully no one was watching.

But then the rest of the scene unfolded in my head.

I stopped dead in my tracks.

What had I done?

Horror flooded me as I heard the echo of my brilliant, after-kiss words.

"Okay, so I gotta go."

And now, as the haze cleared a bit from my brain, I saw how her face had changed and I understood why her eyes had darted downward as her smile crumpled and disappeared.

What the heck was wrong with me? What kind of weirdo kisses someone and then races off like a lunatic?

The Derek Cowell type of weirdo, apparently.

I wondered how long it might take a girl to go from

kissing a guy to never wanting to speak to him again.

I decided not to panic. (I think I'd covered that with the frantic dash out of there anyway.) This was probably fixable, but only if I acted quickly.

Living with three sisters has taught me that the human brain can make a lot of rapid (and not necessarily logical) leaps. I remember once when Kim had this boyfriend named Cal or Carl or something that started with a C (I'm not actually sure about that either) and she broke up with him because he left his watch on the coffee table.

That has to sound crazy. It was. I remember him taking it off to check the back because Kim wanted to know if it was waterproof. He apparently forgot to put it back on and Kim found it after he'd gone home. And here's what happened next.

Kim: Oh, look, Cal (or Carl or whatever) left his watch here.

Everyone else:

(That's right — nada. Because seriously, who cared?)

Kim, looking it over: Hmm. I never heard of this brand before.

Everyone else with any sense:

Paige: Oh, yeah? What kind is it?

Kim: Gubbi.

And then, in case we were all intrigued enough to want to know how it was spelled, she added: G. U. B. B. I.

Any normal person, if they were bored enough to waste the time and energy thinking about it, would have figured it was a lame take on Gucci, and not given it another second's thought. Not Kim. She *pondered* it. The watch, and the brand, and why Cal/Carl/Whatever had left it behind.

One theory she never seemed to consider as she thought her way through this great mystery was that *maybe he just forgot it*.

Nope. This is what Kim's teenage brain came up with: Her boyfriend had left his *watch* — specifically his *Gubbi* watch — as a message to her. And that message was (I am not making this up) it was TIME for them to say GUBBI/GOODBYE. Obviously (to her) he wanted to break up, but couldn't get up the courage to tell her directly.

So, of course, she dumped him first. She didn't ask about the watch, or share her nutty theory with him first either. Straight for the jugular and that was that.

I ran into the poor sap at a skate sharpening shop a couple of days later and when he saw me this sad, hangdog look crept over his face. I could have told him he should be celebrating his escape, but that would have meant talking to him about it. There was *no way* I was risking that kind of conversation.

The scary part of this is that Kim is actually the most level-headed of my sisters. She's not kooky like Paige, or devious like Anna, and yet she went off the rails over a watch!

That worried me. I knew I had to act fast to make sure Denise didn't take my mad dash out of there the wrong way. (Okay, that implies there's a right way to take it. Let's just move along, shall we?)

I pulled out my phone and texted her. It seemed obvious that I needed to apologize and I wasted no time getting right to the point.

Me: Hi Denise. I have no clue why I
did such a dumb thing — sorry!

It seemed like a long time went by, but she finally answered.

So forget it ever happened.

I stared and stared at those five words, trying to feel relieved. There was something making me uneasy, but after I thought it over for a few minutes I decided I was probably just hungry.

I went ahead and texted her back:

Okay, great. :-)

CHAPTER TWENTY-SEVEN

I guess it's pretty clear this is totally new territory to me, this business of kissing and *maybe* having a girl-friend. Since I'm basically clueless about how these things work, that was the biggest question in my head.

Did the kiss mean Denise was my girlfriend? I remember hearing Paige tell one of her friends that she and Junior "just kind of happened." I had no idea what she meant so I put it down to the usual nothingness that comes out of Paige, but maybe it made sense after all. I could be in the middle of a situation exactly like that and not even know it.

Normally, when I wonder anything related to girls I shrug and forget about it. Because I don't usually care enough to go any further than that. Once in a while I might bring something up with Steve, but this wasn't something I wanted to talk to him about. Not until I knew what was up.

And so, I found myself looking for information from

the unlikeliest source ever. My sister Paige.

Since she clearly knew how becoming a couple can "just happen," I decided to ask her a few questions. Nothing obvious — just a casual inquiry or two that might help me figure out my next move with Denise. (Okay, "next move" implies I actually made a first move, which isn't *exactly* true, but still.)

I waited until I found her by herself in the kitchen, sauntered in and plunked down at the counter. I yawned, to show her I was bored, so she'd understand anything I said was of no particular importance.

"Hey, Paige."

She glared at me. Not a great start. I ignored that and pushed ahead.

"How's Junior these days?"

The glare morphed into a clearly suspicious look, where her eyebrows crept closer and closer, and her mouth got small and mean.

"Whaddya mean?" she asked.

"Nothing. I was just wondering."

"You've never wondered anything about Junior before," she pointed out. By now she'd assumed what I can only describe as a combative stance, feet spread and arms crossed in front of her.

"Well, don't flip out, it's no big deal or anything. Can't

a person make conversation around here?"

Paige took a step closer, then another. She jutted her face forward and stared at me fiercely, which I have to say was more than a bit uncomfortable.

"How dumb do you think I am? Something's going on and you *will* tell me what it is."

This was not going the way I'd planned. At all.

"Actually," I said, somehow convincing myself I could still climb out of the hole I was digging, "I was trying to remember how long you guys have been, uh, a couple."

Paige lunged at me, grabbing my T-shirt and almost hauling me off the stool. "You tell me what's going on *right now*!"

"Nothing's going on," I insisted. I tried without success to pull free of her death grip. "Don't be such a psycho."

"Don't lie to me," she yelled into my face. "You've heard something! Now what is it?"

I don't remember ever being afraid of Paige before, but she was definitely scaring me. Her face was red and contorted, her eyes crazed, and she looked capable of ripping me limb from limb if that's what she decided had to be done to make me talk.

"Would you calm down?" I said. It sounded a bit like a whimper.

"DON'T YOU DARE TELL ME TO CALM DOWN!"

Flames began to shoot from her eyes and mouth, or, at least, it looked like they might any second.

At that point I'd have told her *anything* to save myself, but I couldn't because she'd launched into an interrogation of rapid-fire questions that I barely had time to process much less answer.

"He's going to break up with me, isn't he? ISN'T HE?"

"He likes someone else, doesn't he? ANSWER ME!!"

"*Who TOLD YOU?* How long have you known? Does Kim know? Does *everyone* know? Am I the LAST PERSON TO FIND OUT?"

The questions went on and on and on. Sometimes she paused to utter some terrible threat about what she was going to do to Junior when she got her hands on the poor sap.

At some point during the meltdown I realized she'd let go of me so that she could add dramatic gestures to her performance, waving her arms, holding out her hands imploringly, shaking her fist at the non-existent girl who'd come between her and *her* boyfriend.

I felt bad about the trouble I'd accidentally caused for Junior and I knew I should have tried to clear things up, but self-preservation won out. I made a break for it and got the heck out of there.

A while later I told Kim how Paige had gone crazy over

an innocent question and that she was mad at Junior for no reason, in the hope that Kim would be able to talk some sense into her. I figured that left me with a clean conscience.

As for the situation with Denise, I was no further ahead than I'd been before I got Paige all stirred up for nothing. Since I still needed answers, I did something I would normally *never* do — I talked to Mom.

The chance to do that happened right after my folks sat me down to tell me they were lifting my grounding.

"Thanks," I said.

Dad walked over to me and put his hand on my shoulder like he was bestowing some kind of benediction. "You're a good kid, Derek. We've never thought otherwise."

"Okay," I said, and then because it seemed called for, I repeated, "Thanks."

I think he'd have said more, but Mom glanced at her watch and jumped up, saying, "I just have time to get to the drugstore before they close."

"Can I come?"

She looked surprised, but she smiled and said, "Sure. I imagine you're a bit stir-crazy after being stuck in the house."

A moment later, in the car, I took a deep breath and jumped right in.

"Can I ask you something? About, uh, relationships?"

Mom's head jerked a bit, like she was fighting to keep from turning and staring at me. She steadied herself, looked straight ahead and kept her voice totally even when she said, "Of course you can."

"But do you promise you won't tell anyone? Not even Dad?"

She said she wouldn't tell a soul.

"There's this girl," I began. Then I had a bit of trouble putting my thoughts together and that opened up an awkward pause that felt way longer than it actually was. Mom eventually thought I needed a bit of help.

"Steffie?" she said.

That was a surprise. I didn't know Mom had ever suspected I liked Steffie. But now that I'd kissed Denise, whatever I'd felt for Steffie had dissolved like a drifting cloud.

"Naw, that was nothing," I said. Then I told her about Denise. Except I left out the parts that would get me grounded again, such as how I'd been at Steve's place and was hiding from her.

"So, anyway, since we kissed I was wondering if that means we're, you know, automatically a couple, or how that works."

I figured Mom was an expert on this stuff considering

her experience raising three girls, but it took her a minute to answer.

"Do you *want* to be a couple?" she asked first.

"Kind of. I guess."

"Then you'll really need to talk to Denise," she said. "But if you're feeling unsure and you're nervous about bringing it up, you should be able to gauge her feelings on the subject by the way she acts the next time you see her."

I decided that was as good advice as I was going to get.

CHAPTER TWENTY-EIGHT

Having a maybe girlfriend is complicated. I had come to this conclusion by Monday morning based on the number of questions that had been popping into my head over the previous day and a half.

There was the obvious one, which, of course, was whether or not Denise actually *was* my girlfriend, or if we were *about* to be in one of those "just happened" kind of situations I'd been unable to get Paige to explain to me.

That was the tip of the iceberg. I tried Google to find stuff out, but all it did was confuse me more.

I thought I should probably send her a text on Sunday, but when I tried to, I ended up staring vacantly at my phone. I kept hoping she'd send me one first and it seemed maybe she *should* since I'd been the last one to text her yesterday, but that didn't happen.

Then there were questions about what to do at school. Was I supposed to go sit with her at lunch — or ask if she wanted to sit with me and Steve? I knew some couples who were practically glued together, starting with meeting at the lockers in the morning and spending every possible minute together through the day. That didn't exactly appeal to me, but what if it was what Denise expected?

I remember one girl Steve went out with — Gloria Locke, who insisted he had to walk her home from school every day. She lasted until the weather got cold, although I think he might have been losing interest in her anyway. He told me one day just before he broke up with her that she chewed on the ends of her hair. The way he said it, I could tell it grossed him out, which was strange since he'd mentioned that exact same thing when they first became a couple. Except, back then, he seemed to think it was kind of cute.

Well, I don't think Denise chews her hair, but in any case, I'd be okay with walking her home if she wanted me to. It's not very far out of my way and even if it was, I wouldn't mind.

Besides all that, I was kind of wondering when another kiss might happen. Since the first one had been unplanned, I didn't have a lot of confidence in my ability to make a smooth boyfriend move, leaning in for the next one. (I had a *lot* of confidence in my ability to make a fool of myself though, which was kind of a major concern.)

I hoped Mom's advice was good, and that I'd get some signals from Denise about most of this stuff the next time we hung out. For some reason, I thought that was going to happen automatically on Monday. It didn't. In fact, I didn't think she was even at school that day until the second last period when I caught a glimpse of her in the hall.

I'd been keeping an eye out for her — casually I thought, although I may have been a little more obvious than I realized. At lunchtime, Steve asked me if there was something wrong with my neck.

"No, why?" I said.

"You keep cranking your head around like you're working out a kink or something."

"Ha, ha! Working out a kink!" I said. "That's a good one!"

That earned me a lopsided look from him that meant, "What the heck?" I'm sure you've seen the expression.

"You okay?" he asked. He stuffed a chocolate chip muffin into his mouth and bit off half of it while he waited for me to answer.

"Sure," I said, resisting the urge to take another look around for Denise.

Steve might have kept digging into the cause of my

strange behavior, but Tamrah Kingston was going by our table just then. This totally distracted him.

It distracted me too, but not the same way. The thought barged into my head that if I could have either Tamrah or Denise as my girlfriend, I would pick Denise. That was the moment I knew I didn't just like her, I liked her a *lot*.

Realizing this made me feel, I dunno, sort of queasy and kind of miserable. (That's not something I planned to tell her, although, after hearing how I raced off at breakneck speed after kissing her, it might not seem entirely out of the question.)

I needed to see her. To talk to her. To find out for sure if she liked me back. (Two days ago I'd have said yes, but by this point *nothing* seemed clear.) Mostly, I just wanted to stand beside her, as goofy as that probably sounds.

When I finally saw her near the end of the day, I tried to get her attention, but she was hurrying to one of her classes and the one I was going to was in a different direction.

So, after school I kept an eye out, planning to casually fall in beside her when she started for home, but she must have gone out one of the side exits.

I left dejectedly, dragging my feet as I walked along.

I suddenly knew it was no accident that I hadn't seen Denise all day. She was avoiding me. I'd blown it on Saturday and there was never going to be another chance. There was nothing to do now but accept it and move on.

So I'm not sure why I found myself on the sidewalk in front of her place ten minutes later. Revisiting the scene of the crime maybe? I trudged by slowly, turned around at the corner and moseyed past again.

After I'd passed by the second time, I told myself I'd better knock it off.

"Go home," I muttered to myself. "What are you, some kind of nut-job stalker?"

I made it a block and a half before I did an about-face and went back. It was like my feet were working against me, forcing me along that sidewalk.

The fourth time I was making my way by her house Denise burst out the front door and stomped halfway down the driveway where she stopped, fists on hips, and asked just exactly what I thought I was doing.

"I don't know," I admitted.

"Are you trying to be funny?" she said angrily.

I didn't know how to answer that, so I didn't try. "I was looking for you at school today," I said instead. "It seemed like you might be avoiding me."

"Well, why wouldn't I?" she said. "And anyway, what

do you care?"

Obviously, she was still super steamed about Saturday. Maybe, I thought, I hadn't apologized enough.

"I really meant it when I said I was sorry," I told her. "I don't know *why* I took off like that."

Denise stopped glowering at me. Her mouth opened and closed a couple of times, and she dropped her hands to her sides. She even unclenched her fists.

"What?" she asked.

I repeated what I'd just said.

"You *idiot*, Derek," she said. But she was smiling and walking toward me and I somehow knew that this was about the best thing I could have hoped for.

Chapter Twenty-Nine

So it's official. I *do* have a girlfriend.

Turns out the thing to do in this kind of situation is to talk, not to your sister, or to your mother, but to the girl herself.

Denise explained that to me. She rolled her eyes a lot and elbowed me in the ribs twice while she was talking, but her eyes were shiny and happy.

Also — and I won't personally need this for future reference because believe me, I've learned my lesson, but it might help someone else — when you tell a girl you're sorry about something, make sure you also tell her *what*. Otherwise, there could be a misunderstanding that will ruin everything, which almost happened to us.

See, when I texted Denise that I was sorry, I meant I was sorry for taking off so suddenly afterward, but *she* took it a completely different way.

"I thought you were sorry we kissed," she said.

"No way!" I blurted. "That was great!"

Denise laughed. Then her smile disappeared behind a kind of shy, serious look.

"Does that mean you like me?" she asked.

I remembered Steve telling me one time you always had to keep them guessing and you should never give a girl ammunition like that. I decided to risk it anyway.

"I like you a *lot*," I said.

Denise's smile came back in full force. Then she told me she liked me a lot too. So I asked her, did she want to be my girlfriend and she *did*.

Looks like Steve's theories on women could use some updating. Not that I was ever going to tell him any of this.

If this was a typical story, it would end here. All the crazy events that were first set in motion by an accidental photobomb had led me on this path to Denise. We'd have reached a happy ending, and who doesn't like that?

Unfortunately, it wasn't quite over.

The first part of the week went great. After I left Denise's place on Monday, I took a few minutes to stop in at Steve's and fill him in on the news.

His mom answered the door. She seemed to be in a cranky mood judging by her expression. It was the way you might look if you were expecting a pizza delivery and someone showed up at your door with a steaming plate of dog barf.

She didn't wait for me to speak, just hollered, "Steve! Derek is here!"

Then she walked away, leaving the door open and me standing on the outside. Steve's head poked around the corner a minute later. He motioned me in and we walked silently to his room. Neither of us spoke until he shut the door, and then we kept our voices low.

"What's with your mom?" I asked.

"She got dumped, like, ten minutes ago. The guy — I think his name was Mitchell — was supposed to take her out for supper and instead he texts her and tells her they're through."

"That's pretty mean."

"Yeah. She *was* going to give me money to get a meatball sub. Now I'll be lucky if I can sneak into the kitchen for a bowl of cereal. I mean, I feel bad for her, but who wants to listen to that kind of sob story from their *mother*?"

"She sure has lousy luck with guys," I said.

Steve shrugged. I couldn't blame him. I wouldn't want to talk about my mother's dating life either, if she had one. Time to change the subject.

"Anyway, I just stopped by to tell you something." I paused for a couple of seconds. "I'm, uh, seeing someone."

He looked confused.

"You mean, like a ghost?" he said.

Not the first reaction I'd expected. On the other hand, I'd never had a girlfriend before and this had come about pretty suddenly. I got that it might not have seemed like the obvious conclusion. Still, it was hard to believe a ghost was his top guess.

"No, a girl."

He laughed. He said, "No, seriously."

"I *am* serious."

As it sank in that I was telling the truth a grin spread across Steve's face. That was followed by the obligatory punch on the shoulder.

"You dawg!" he said. "You've been holding out on me. Who is it?"

"Denise Peeters."

"No kidding," he said, but it wasn't a question. I could see on his face how that made sense to him. Denise wasn't *his* type, but if *I* liked her, that was fine with him.

That might sound a bit insulting, but I got it. I'd felt the same way about a couple of the girls he'd liked. One of them laughed at *everything*. Honestly, every single thing. And another one pawed at her hair compulsively like she was trying to shake out bugs. They might have *looked* good, but it ended there.

Denise was funny and smart and pretty and really, really nice. Every time I thought about her, I felt good.

Of course, word travels fast and I only made it to Wednesday before news of my status as a non-single guy reached my house. It was, not surprisingly, Paige who heard it first, since she goes to my school. Even though we have different lunch hours and are able to mostly avoid each other, things trickle down.

"Derek has a girlfriend," she announced, meeting Mom as she came through the door after work.

Mom gave me the slightest nod and a silent message passed between us. All she said to Paige was, "That's nice." Then she went to the kitchen to see what Dad was making for supper.

But Kim and Anna, who had been nowhere in sight, appeared instantly, clamoring for details.

Paige had none. Probably because there were none to be had. The announcement was the whole story and after asking me a couple dozen annoying questions, which I ignored, the three of them gave up.

By Thursday it was already starting to feel natural seeing myself as a guy with a girlfriend. Denise and her friend Sharon were joining me and Steve at our table at lunch and it was looking like Steve and Sharon might "just sort of happen."

It was mostly nice having lunch with the girls. The only drawback was remembering to be on guard. I didn't think my new girlfriend would be too impressed if I blurted something out with food in my mouth or belched like a Neanderthal.

CHAPTER THIRTY

Less than a week later, fate decided it was time to mess with me again.

It was my sisters who alerted me to the problem. Not on purpose, but I like to think they might have warned me even if I hadn't accidentally overheard their conversation.

Kim was in her favorite chair in the TV room and Paige was standing next to her, leaning down. I was on the couch listening to some tunes and wouldn't normally have paid them the slightest attention. But then I heard Kim clearly say my name during a break between songs.

It made me curious enough to pause the next song, but I kept the earbuds in and my head down so they wouldn't know I was paying attention.

"Should we tell him?" Paige asked.

"I dunno," Kim said, turning the "no" part into two singsong syllables. "He's *not* going to be happy."

I might not be, but Paige seemed, if not happy, at least

entertained. She giggled and said, "That's for sure. He's going to *lose* it."

I slowly shifted my gaze toward them. They were both focused on Kim's phone.

Something clenched into a tight ball in the pit of my stomach. I un-slouched from the corner of the couch and tugged the buds out of my ears.

"What's going on?" I asked.

The girls turned to face me in a single motion. Their faces were a slideshow of surprise, guilt, and maybe just a tinge of pity.

"There's a new video," Paige said, trying to look indignant. "It's the WORST! I even feel kind of bad for you."

I yanked myself to my feet and crossed the room to where she was sitting. A glance at Kim's phone (and the way my own started to light up) was enough to tell me the worst had indeed happened. It was the rooftop video from the train station. The one Riley had *promised* not to share with anyone. The one Riley claimed she'd erased from her phone.

My very first thought was that *Denise* would see it. I felt a shudder running up my spine.

It was true that she'd been super cool about the other videos, but we hadn't been a couple then. I doubted she'd be excited to have the whole town reminded of what a gutless wimp her boyfriend was.

There was more to it than that, though. It was the thought of how *she* was going to see *me*. Sure, she knew I'd been scared up there, that I'd had to be rescued, but *knowing* that and actually *seeing* it were two different things.

I lost count of the number of times I started to text her that evening, never quite managing to hit send. What stopped me was knowing she *had* to have seen the video by then. There was no way it was out there being shared all over Breval without someone sending it to my girlfriend. (Goodness knows there was no shortage of people sending it to ME!)

So, if Denise had seen it, as I was sure she had, why hadn't she messaged me?

I could only think of one reason. She was embarrassed.

I could also only think of one person to blame.

Riley. Just the thought of her made me furious.

I spent a good half hour seething, and thinking about how she was *not* going to get away with this. She might think this move of hers had given her the upper hand between us, but she was going to find out just how wrong she was, and soon.

Not that I had any sort of actual plan to make her pay. Not at first. There was just the idea that she must!

And another thing. It puzzled me, trying to figure out what her strategy might be, what the motive was for what she'd just done. She'd thrown away the only ammunition she had to keep me from telling everyone the truth about her. Or, at least, as much of the truth as I knew.

Maybe she'd convinced herself that if she humiliated me, she could claim I was making things up to get back at her — if I retaliated and exposed her as a total liar.

If so, that miscalculation was going to backfire on her, and badly. A plan was slowly forming in my brain.

A plan for revenge.

That festered and grew until bedtime, when another thought managed to slip through. As I was lying back on my pillow with my arms crossed behind my head, I couldn't help wishing my life could go back to the way it used to be.

When no one is paying attention to you, you can klutz your way along and never give a thought to your reputation. Heck, you don't even *have* a reputation. Nobody's watching, because when people barely know you exist, they don't care if you make a fool of yourself now and then.

But that felt like the way my world (and life) had been in another lifetime. Ever since the first picture got out there — the accidental photobomb — people were paying attention.

And no one cuts you any slack, that's for sure, which was something else I'd learned. This town was about as fickle as a place could be.

The only person I knew for sure I could count on was Steve. I was hoping the same was true for Denise, but that wasn't looking too hopeful at the moment.

CHAPTER THIRTY-ONE

I expected the worst at school the next morning so the reception I got didn't shock me.

It was a collage of mockery. I might even have been impressed at the variety of ways my schoolmates found to ridicule me if their actual performances hadn't been so predictable.

There were those who contorted their faces to appear terrified and others who trembled in supposed fear — these two groups made up the majority. But there were a few more original acts: the whimperers, screechers, frozen statues, and even a few who hit the floor and pretended to cling to it.

Some kids just laughed. Some looked embarrassed for me. Some shouted out what they probably thought were hilarious bits of commentary.

For the most part, it was actually boring. I'd already decided how to handle what I'd known was coming, so I put on a grin, forced out a few fake laughs and acted like

I wasn't one bit bothered.

And then it hit me. I actually *didn't* care very much about any of what was happening!

What I cared about was Denise, and what was going on with her. So I was nervous when I finally spotted her coming toward me from the south entrance. I suddenly felt as if an enormous rock was sitting in my gut.

As she came fully into view, I saw that she was chatting with another girl who was walking next to her.

She must have sensed me looking at her then, because her eyes shifted up, over and straight at me.

No smile. Her face was instantly serious and as she got closer, she leaned toward me and said, very quietly, "It's almost time for the bell. We'll talk at lunch, okay?"

It was not a good morning. Classes stretched on and on, time shifted into slow motion mode, and the furtive ridicule from my classmates grew more annoying and tiresome by the moment.

It seemed lunch would never arrive. And then it did and I wished with everything in me that I could delay it for even a few more minutes.

Until we sat down face to face, Denise was still my girlfriend. More than that, I could hope she wasn't going to dump me. Except, I *knew* she was. I'm not an intuitive guy, but this was one of those premonitions you get when you're one hundred percent sure about what's going to happen.

I dragged my feet toward the cafeteria, hoping she'd chosen a remote corner table where there'd be a bit of privacy.

Nope. She and Sharon were already at the table with Steve. They all looked up as I got close, prompted by the murmurs around them. I wondered, without really caring, how long ridicule season was going to last.

I took the seat across from Denise and offered what I hoped was a brave smile, although brave wasn't a word much associated with me these days.

Denise's face was solemn. She reached over, touched my hand lightly and said, "I'm really sorry, Derek."

And there it was. I almost felt relief. At least she hadn't dragged it out with a long explanation or told me we were better as friends or whatever.

"It's okay," I managed. "I don't blame you at all."

"Why would you blame *me*?" she asked, surprised. "I didn't send the video all over the place."

"No, I mean—"

What *did* I mean? I searched my brain for words. Nothing. Thanks brain.

"Well, anyway," she said when it was apparent I had

no immediate plans to finish my sentence. "I was furious when I saw the video this morning. Whoever sent it was just plain mean."

"You just saw it *today*?" I said.

"Yup. My phone was missing last night," she said. "I thought I left it in my locker, but then Dad found it in the car this morning."

"Oh," I said, as that sank in. So, her silence yesterday had meant nothing.

"I feel so bad for you," she said. "It's like the whole train station thing was over and done, and now this."

"So you're *not* breaking up with me?" I said.

Denise laughed. Beside her, Sharon laughed too.

"You've gotta be kidding," Sharon said. "Denise would never do something like that. She's the most loyal person I know."

I felt my face redden.

"Never mind," Denise said. "I'm just impressed with how you're handling it."

"I'm not letting it get to me," I said, which I think came across as pretty manly.

"I wish we could find out who did it, though," she said. "I'd love to tell them what I think of them."

"I bet it was meant as a joke," Steve said.

I was annoyed, but not exactly surprised to hear him sticking up for Riley. Cute girls get cut a lot of slack in his rule book.

Denise shook her head. "A joke is funny — that was anything but," she said, offering me an onion ring from her lunch tray.

Steve shrugged and dropped it. I wish I could say the same for the rest of the students at Breval Middle School. The taunting went on for the remainder of the day and it was a relief to head home after the final bell.

My sisters had pretty much gotten it out of their system already so there wasn't too much said at home. Until Anna found me getting myself a bedtime snack and took that opportunity to have a chat.

I'd been dotting butter on a crispy brown toaster waffle when she slid onto the chair directly across from me.

"Someone in my class said you wet your pants," she announced. "On the roof that day."

Terrific. More rumors.

"Well I didn't," I told her. "If I had, everyone would have seen it in the videos taken on the ground."

A smile burst onto her face. (And was that actually *relief*? Good to know my own sister had found the pants-wetting story credible.)

"That's what I told Gertie," she said.

It took me a few seconds to remember that Gertie was one of Anna's friends. If I had the right kid in mind, she was a gangly girl with stringy hair who sounded like a seal when she laughed.

"Well, good news. You can go ahead and brag to Gertie — heck, tell *all* your friends — that your brother doesn't go around wetting himself," I said.

"I'll just tell Gertie. She's the only one who will care," Anna told me. "She loves you. She thinks you're cute."

My stomach lurched at the thought those words coming out of my sister's *nine-year-old* friend.

"Stop it," I said. "Don't be saying stuff like that."

"But it's true," Anna said indignantly. "She told me!"

"I said stop!" I almost shouted. "That's disgusting!"

"My friends are *not* disgusting," Anna said angrily.

"That's not what I meant. But they're way too young to be talking that way about guys. Especially if the guy is me."

Anna gave me a cold, hard look. She was still sulking when I swallowed the last bite of my waffle and escaped.

I shook off the grossness of *that* conversation by letting my mind wander to thoughts of revenge on Riley. Specifically, to the plan that had been festering since the first moment the video was shared.

CHAPTER THIRTY-TWO

When my phone alarm woke me the next morning I only groaned once before I remembered. It was rec center day. Community service time.

Instantly energized, I was out of bed and downstairs in a flash. I gobbled down some cereal, jogged upstairs to shower and brush my teeth, threw on some clothes and headed cheerfully out the door. You'd have thought I was on my way to do something fun with my friends instead of spending the day on my knees with a scrub bucket.

Of course, it wasn't the cleaning I was looking forward to. It was putting Part One of my plan of revenge in place. I could hardly wait to see Riley's face when she realized what a huge mistake she'd made.

I got there first this time, and went straight to the office where I was treated to the sight of Mr. Durand wolfing down a couple of breakfast burritos. He had a certain rhythm going, which was, bite, chew, chew, swallow, gulp a mouthful of coffee, repeat.

He waved me in and pointed to a chair without the slightest break in this pattern. I waited until he was finished before saying good morning to him.

"Hey kid." He glanced sideways at a form sitting just out of danger from the burrito drips that had plopped onto a napkin on the middle of the desk. "Derek, right?"

"Yes, sir."

"And call me Serge, remember?"

"Okay."

"So, you raring to go this morning?"

"Sure," I said.

He laughed. "Probably raring to go *back to bed*," he said. "But I'm glad to see you're being a good sport."

A squeak behind us announced Riley's arrival and a few seconds later she was standing in the office doorway. She gave me a half wave, which I ignored.

Serge pushed his chair back. He stood and brushed crumbs from his shirt before leading us along the hall to the janitor's supply room. He passed out the supplies we needed and told us to go ahead and finish up the job we'd started last weekend.

I noticed Riley darting quick glances at me as we carried our buckets and cleaning stuff to the auditorium. It was obvious she was expecting me to say something about the video, but I kept my mouth shut and got straight to work as soon as I found the spot I'd stopped at the previous Saturday.

We worked in a tight, tense silence for more than an hour. That took some self-control, believe me. There were a few times I was tempted to speak up, but I wanted to force her to start the conversation.

Finally, she got up, stretched and said, "I'm going to get a bottle of water. You want one?"

I don't know what I was expecting from her, but that sure wasn't it. I stopped scrubbing at a glob of unknown grime and turned toward her.

"Well, well," I said. "I have to say I'm a bit surprised that you're offering to do something *nice* for me."

Riley sighed, like we'd been arguing for a long time and she was sick of it.

"You want some water or not?" she repeated.

I tried to think of something else to say, something clever and cutting that would draw her into a conversation about the video, and that she couldn't sidestep so easily.

Nothing.

"Yeah, okay," I said. Because I *was* kind of thirsty and I knew I'd look like a fool if I refused and then two minutes later went and got myself a bottle. Which I'd definitely have to do, since nothing makes you thirstier than thinking about a nice cold drink when you don't have one.

By the time she got back with the water I'd grown suspicious. When she passed one of the bottles to me I checked carefully to make sure the seal wasn't broken. It seemed fine.

"Anyway," she said. "Thanks for not saying anything."

Her words registered slowly, like I was hearing them spoken through a cardboard tube.

This was her master plan for getting on my good side?

"You're *not* serious," I said. "You think you can act half civil to me for two minutes and I'm going to forget about what you did?"

Riley shifted from foot to foot. Her eyes swept over me as though she was examining a big hairy spider.

"If you mean the video," she said at last. "That wasn't me."

I almost laughed out loud. Did she think I was going to take *her* word for anything? I'd only known her a short time and the collection of lies — and those were just the ones I *knew* about — were already a mile high. This was definitely a no-brainer.

"Don't waste your time lying," I said. "I know the truth."

"Believe whatever you want," she said. The hostility was back in full force, curling the edge of her lip and casting an ugly shadow on her face.

"I'll do a lot more than that," I told her. "And you know what they say about payback."

"I don't care," she said, but her voice wavered and the sneer was gone.

There wasn't another word exchanged between us that day. I did a bit of talking to myself, though, kind of thinking out loud.

"I wonder who should I tell *first*," I said.

And, "What do they call someone who can't tell the truth? Oh, right, a pathological liar."

It wasn't quite as satisfying as I'd hoped it would be. After our conversation, Riley turned stone-faced and offered no reaction to anything else I said. Even so, I knew she heard me. Believing she was about to be exposed had to be worrying her.

That was the first part of the plan. To have her waiting, with her nerves on edge, for when it was going to happen.

What I hadn't yet figured out was what, if anything, to do next. Because I'm not a rat. I wanted Riley to *think* I was going to leak her secret, but there was no way I was really going to do it.

In any case, this seemed like enough for now. Let her sweat.

CHAPTER THIRTY-THREE

The next thing that happened took place on Sunday, although I didn't hear about it until Monday evening when Kim got a phone call. I don't know what was happening on the other end of the call, but there was quite a performance on hers. Gasping, pacing, head-grabbing (her own, thankfully) and cries of things like "No!" and "I can't believe it."

By the time Kim got off the phone our whole family had gathered around and was waiting to find out what was going on. She faced us solemnly and tried to keep her voice steady.

"Riley is *gone*," she said, and burst into tears.

The awfulness of those words cascaded over me. I couldn't move; I could barely breathe.

It felt as though all the air had been sucked out of the room. Riley was dead and I knew without a second's hesitation that *I was responsible*.

What had I done?

Mom stepped forward and pulled Kim gently into her arms.

"Oh, honey," she said. "What happened?"

"Nobody knows," Kim sobbed. "I just can't believe it. I mean, where would she go?"

Huh?

Where would she go?

Mom stepped back a bit, still holding onto Kim, but by the shoulders as she looked into her face.

"Do you mean this girl has run off somewhere?" she asked.

Kim nodded, sniffling and pulling herself together.

"Well, for goodness' sakes! I thought you were saying something happened to her."

"Me too!" I blurted, partly angry, but mostly relieved. That drew a few strange looks.

"What do you care?" Kim snapped. "You don't even like Riley."

"So what? That doesn't mean I want her going around dying," I said. I would normally have left the room after a lame comment like that, but I wanted to find out if Kim knew anything else. She did, though it wasn't much.

"She disappeared on Sunday when the rest of the family was having lunch at Have Happy."

"They have a lunch buffet on the weekend," Dad said,

which had nothing to do with anything. "I wonder why they didn't take her with them."

"They asked her, but she said she wasn't feeling good and she wanted to stay home and lie down. Except, when they got back, she was gone."

"Maybe someone kidnapped her," Anna said. Not the conclusion most people would jump to right off the bat, but, as our resident criminal, Anna has her own way of seeing things.

Kim glared at her. "Some of her stuff was gone, so they know she ran off. But now she's been missing for more than twenty-four hours and who knows what's happened to her."

"She could be starving to death," Paige suggested. I'm sure she thought that was somehow helpful.

"I think that would take more than a day," Mom said. "Anyway, I'm going to call Trisha's mother to see if there's anything we can do. She must be worried sick about her niece. And goodness knows how she's going to contact the girl's parents!"

I slunk out of there.

So, she wasn't dead, which was good, but a missing teen is no joke either. Besides which, it was still my fault, so I wasn't feeling too proud.

I wondered if Trisha's mother was going to tell Mom

the truth that Riley wasn't actually her niece. Not that any of us would ever hear about it if she did.

The next half hour saw me searching social media sites to see if I could find a way to connect with Riley, assuming she had her phone with her. I thought if I could reach her, I could make this whole mess go away by letting her know I'd never really have ratted her out. No luck.

Then it occurred to me that Kim might have her number. I couldn't just ask for it though — not without raising a lot of questions. I'd have to find a way to get my hands on Kim's phone.

That was possibly the most dangerous mission I'd ever undertaken. Kim once threw me on the entryway floor and bent my arm up behind my back until I cried. (Don't judge me, you weren't there.) And that was because she caught me with my hand in her jacket pocket, sneaking a piece of gum.

I didn't even want to think about what she'd do if she caught me with her phone. Instead, I steadied my nerves and went back downstairs, formulating a plan as I went. Kim's phone is practically an extension of her. If it's not in her hand, it's somewhere on her person. She wouldn't take two steps away from that thing unless she was tricked into it.

In retrospect, I should have spent a bit more time on

the plan, even though it worked up to a point. I waited until she sat the phone on the arm of her chair, then sauntered to the front door, looked out the glass and yelled, "Hey! Is that Luna Amatulli?"

Paige and Kim threw themselves from their chairs, hurled themselves to the door, yanked it open and flung themselves outside. As they did that, I dashed back in and grabbed Kim's phone.

"Whatcha doing?"

I jumped about six hundred feet and almost dropped it, which would have been my life!

Anna!

I'd somehow overlooked her, and the fact that she finds all the hoopla over Luna Amatulli boring. She hadn't budged from the couch.

"Nothing," I said.

She smiled the smile of the happy blackmailer. There was no way I was getting out of this one scot-free.

But there was no time to worry about that now! I scrolled frantically through Kim's contacts. Once, twice, three times. No Riley. The sound of the door closing told me I was out of time and I dropped the phone back where it had been. A split-second later Kim and Paige and their angry faces re-entered the room.

"What's the big idea?" Paige demanded. Had she *really*

expected the reclusive Luna to be strolling casually along our street?

I gave the fakest laugh in the history of fake laughs. Until Kim spoke.

"*Who was touching my phone?*"

Her tone was totally calm and flat, which sent a chill up my quaking spine.

"I, uh, it was, that is, I just—"

Kim was advancing on me and in my panic I did something totally bizarre.

I told the truth.

Or, at least, part of it. I told her I'd been looking for Riley's number.

"I was embarrassed to ask for it because I knew I'd have to admit why," I explained. "I said something mean to her the other day and I wanted to let her know I was sorry."

Kim was barely an inch away from me by then, leaning in, eyebrows practically touching. She paused and I could see she was deciding whether or not I'd been telling the truth.

And then she hugged me.

I could hardly believe it. Not only was I off the hook with Kim, but Anna's face told me she knew she'd lost her ammunition against me.

I felt great, until I remembered Riley was still missing. And I still didn't have her number.

Then I thought of Steve, which I should have done in the first place. He definitely had Riley's number since she'd sent him the video. I shot him a quick text.

I need Riley's number.

His answer was back in seconds.

What do you want it for?

I was halfway through answering when something stopped me.

Steve also had the video. What if Riley had been telling the truth when she *insisted* it wasn't her who sent it out?

Could my best friend have done it? Was that even *possible*?

I backspaced the message I'd begun and wrote instead:

Actually, never mind

Things started running through my head. For starters, there was the way Steve obviously felt left out when I suddenly became popular. But there was more than that. He'd been angry about the picture with Skylah, and his reaction to the photo with Luna Amatulli hadn't been great, especially when he got cut right out of it when it was posted on *Strandz*.

I also couldn't help remembering the way he'd practically defended whoever sent out the rooftop video. As if it was nothing but a harmless joke.

And one other thing poked its way into my head — the disappointment in Steve's voice the day he'd said no one would ever see him skywalking. Well, they'd seen him now, even if the focus moved to my terror afterward.

Then I laughed right out loud. What was wrong with me? How could I think for one minute that Steve would do something like that to me? I knew the guy. I'd known him my whole life.

There was *no way* he had anything to do with that video being shared all over Breval.

CHAPTER THIRTY-FOUR

Two more days went by with no sign of Riley. Kim kept us updated on what was happening. Or rather, what wasn't happening.

There was talk at school and talk just about everywhere you went. And sightings! There were enough sightings for two or three Rileys, but none of them turned up anything other than a few interesting stories.

One old fellow claimed she was asleep out behind the shed in his backyard. The police checked into that only to find the neighbor's German Shepherd there, along with three new puppies.

Then a nineteen-year-old girl working nights at a drive-through claimed a girl matching Riley's description had approached the window on foot and asked for something to eat. She later admitted she'd made the story up in case there was a reward. I don't know how she thought she'd qualify for a reward by telling a pointless story, even if there had been one.

I listened carefully to everything, hoping for a grain of truth or a hint that would help me figure out where she was. I couldn't focus in class and even had a hard time paying attention to Denise when we ate lunch.

Tuesday felt like it would never end and by the time school let out on Wednesday I couldn't take it any longer. In an act of pure desperation, I walked over to Trisha's house instead of going home. She answered my knock.

"Hi, Derek."

"Hi, Trisha. I was looking for Riley's phone number."

"What for?"

"There's something I want to tell her. I think it might help."

Trisha recited a number.

"Whoa, hold on!" I pulled out my phone and input the number as she repeated it slowly.

"It won't help though," she added when I'd input Riley to my contacts. "She took out the battery."

I wondered why she hadn't started off with that detail, which seemed pretty significant, but a deeper question came to mind.

"How do you know that?"

"The police told my dad. They said the last time her phone pinged she was somewhere near the dental clinic."

"What day was that?"

"Sunday. It hasn't been on since. That's how they figured she took out the battery."

It wasn't much of a starting point, but it was all I had. I made my mind up to head that way after supper. Once I'd done my chore for the day, which was loading the dishwasher and wiping the table and counters, I told Mom I was going for a walk. She smiled and winked and told me to have a really nice time.

I realized she assumed I was going to see Denise, which was actually a great idea. I texted her and she agreed to meet up with me at the end of her street.

She was already at the corner when I got there. Plus she was holding two big, fat oatmeal raisin cookies. She passed both of them over.

"Don't you want one?" I asked. I tried not to sound pushy about it.

Denise laughed. "I actually had four with me when I left the house," she said, patting her stomach happily.

In spite of that, I thought she was looking a bit too fondly at the unbitten cookie in my free hand so I dropped it to my side and out of her line of vision. No point taking unnecessary risks.

"So, where are we going?"

"Just for a walk," I said, which wasn't a lie, but also wasn't exactly the whole truth.

She didn't ask anything else, not then anyway. We started walking and she was close enough that our arms brushed sometimes. Every so often she looked over and smiled at me and I liked that.

When we got to the dental clinic, I found myself looking around, trying to think of where Riley might have been heading when she came this way. The clinic is at the top of a hill near the outskirts on the south side of town, which offered a great view. Unfortunately, that's all it offered.

"Are you looking for something, Derek?" Denise asked, breaking into my thoughts.

"Kind of."

"Is this about Riley?"

I sure hadn't expected that. "How did you know?"

"You've been super distracted since she went missing." She turned slowly, making a circle, her hand shading her eyes as she peered around. "So, why here?"

I explained what Trisha had told me earlier. "I know that was three days ago, but I had some crazy idea I might get a hint about where she was going."

"Nothing, huh?"

I shook my head. And then I blurted it out, how I'd found something out about Riley and had told her I was going to spread it around because of what she'd done.

"I think that's why she took off," I finished.

"What do you mean, about what Riley did?"

"The video on the roof of the train station," I said. "She's the one who posted it."

"Did she tell you that?"

"No, she tried to deny it, but it had to be her. She *made* the video, and the only other person she sent it to was Steve. Until last week."

Denise frowned. She looked like she was about to say something else when a thought flashed in my brain.

"I have an idea!" I said excitedly.

"About where she is?"

"Yeah — come on!"

I hurried down a path to a lower street with Denise right behind me. Ten minutes later we'd crossed through to a now-familiar sight in town.

The old train station.

"I just remembered, that day when we were on the roof, Riley said she felt safe from the whole world," I told Denise.

Denise stared at me. "And?" she said.

"So, I think she might be there."

"On the roof?"

"Maybe. Or inside — it would be an ideal place to hide out."

"But you're already in trouble over this place," Denise said. "Imagine what would happen if you got caught in there again. Besides, you can't go on the roof."

She was polite enough not to mention that I became a human jellyfish up there.

"I *have* to check," I said.

"Okay then," Denise said. "I'll stay here and keep watch. If I see anyone coming I'll send you a text to get out quick."

Ten minutes later I was making my way up to the door onto the roof. I moved as quietly as the creaky old wooden steps would allow and when I reached the top I slowly eased the door open.

And there she was, not ten feet away. She looked so small, sitting cross-legged and hunched over, swaying slightly and singing a low, mournful song.

Chapter Thirty-Five

I tapped gently on the doorframe. Riley stiffened for a second and then swung around slowly.

"Hi," I said.

"This is *not* really happening," she said.

"I need to talk to you," I said, trying to ignore the way she irritated me, even when I was trying to rescue her.

"So talk." She stood and smirked. "You're welcome to join me out here."

Normally, this would be the place in the story where the hero overcomes his fear and walks right out, proving how determined he really is to do the right thing.

But not in my story.

"I can't," I said. "I'm way too afraid of heights."

I expected her to make fun of me, and I think she was going to — at first. Her chin lifted and her eyes were mocking, but when she opened her mouth, something stopped her.

Her face changed. Slowly, like the scorn was melting

away. And the next thing I knew, she was sobbing.

I did take a single step forward, because it seemed the decent thing to do would be to go to her and give her a shoulder to cry on or something. It was impossible. I couldn't make it past the doorframe, or even let go of it.

"Um, you want to come inside?" I said, feeling awkward and embarrassed.

To my surprise, she stumbled forward, nodding, and followed me inside to the landing. Since I didn't have a clue what she was crying about, I just waited for her to speak. When she did, it was nothing I expected her to say.

"I've never been that brave," she said.

"Huh?" I said.

A smile trembled on her face for a microsecond, and was gone.

"Brave enough to *admit* I was afraid of anything," she said. "I could never do that."

"Is that why you make stuff up?" I said. It was a bit of a wild guess, but for once I got something right.

"That's *exactly* why," she said. She looked, I dunno, a bit amazed, at my insightfulness, I suppose.

"I figured," I said. And nodded wisely.

"I always feel there's too much risk in telling the truth, that if they know the facts people will look down on me, and I won't have any friends."

Then she told me a bunch of stuff about herself and her family and I could see why she might not want to go around broadcasting some of it. It's her business, so I won't say any more about it, but it put her in a completely different light.

When she was finished talking, she said, very softly, "Please don't tell anyone."

"That's why I'm here," I said. "I wanted to let you know I wasn't really going to do that. I just said it because I was upset about the video."

"I told you I didn't do that," she reminded me.

"Yeah, but you make things up," I said. "So I didn't believe you."

Then I smiled to show her I wasn't mad about it anymore. That only made her stick her chin forward and some of the blaze came back to her eyes.

"I *said*, it *wasn't me*!" she repeated.

And I knew, right then and there, she was telling the truth.

That only left one possible culprit. *Steve*. The friend I'd been so sure could never have done such a thing.

But I had no time to think about that right then. Riley needed to go home, and I was going to persuade her to do just that no matter how long it took.

It didn't take long. I think she was hungry and tired

and probably lonely after days hiding out by herself. But she was also nervous about facing everyone, which made her more than willing to have Denise and I walk her home.

Man, were they glad to see her! There were hugs and tears and more hugs — it looked like it might go on for a while so Denise and I snuck off before we got dragged into the whole emotion-fest.

It was a nice night and after the Riley rescue we both felt lit-up happy. It would have been sweet to just keep walking for a while, but I needed to settle this thing with Steve.

I explained that to Denise and then walked her to her place.

"Good luck, Derek," she said, leaning up and giving me a quick kiss. It landed kind of lopsided, half on and half off my mouth, which made her giggle.

I hated leaving her. But this had to be taken care of, and putting it off was only going to make it worse.

Confrontation isn't really my thing so I don't have a lot of practice. If there's such a thing as the right way to accuse a person of something, it's probably not what I did. I went straight to Steve's house and knocked good and hard on the door.

"Why'd you do it?" I asked as soon as Steve appeared.

"Do what?" He looked puzzled.

"Don't waste your time with the innocent act," I said. "I know you're the one who sent that video out."

Steve blinked a couple of times, as if he was trying to bring things into focus. Then he looked me in the face, man to man, and his hands came up, like he was surrendering. For a second I expected him to blurt out a confession.

He didn't.

"Whoa!" he said. "Is this a joke?"

"Why don't you just admit it?" I said. "In a way, I even get why you did it. Like you said, it was the only way anyone was ever going to see you skywalking."

I thought I was going easy on him, not bringing up the jealousy part of his motive, but apparently Steve saw it differently. He took a step back and slammed the door in my face.

It was my turn to stand there blinking. A minute passed, maybe two, before I knew for sure the door was staying shut. I turned and headed home.

By the time I reached my place I wished I hadn't said anything. Who knew how long Steve was going to stay mad.

And what if things were never the way they were before? What difference did it make, really? None of the people making fun of me were my actual friends. I knew that. So what if Steve made a dumb mistake? I should have waited for him to tell me the truth whenever he was ready. And if he never was, so what?

Trying to make him own up to what he did wasn't worth anything. At all.

Chapter Thirty-Six

I decided, after a few lousy days, that maybe I should apologize to Steve.

The first time I thought of doing that, it seemed weird, because I wasn't the one who should be saying I was sorry. Yes, I'd done the wrong thing confronting him, but he'd started it when he humiliated me all over town. Of the two wrong things, his was definitely bigger.

So that day, I did nothing. I also did nothing the second day, for the same reason.

The third day I decided not to think about it at all. Fortunately, I have a girlfriend.

Denise had some stuff to take to the shelter, so of course I'd offered to go with her and carry anything that was heavy.

"Do you think Anna might like to join us?" she asked.

"She wouldn't be much help," I pointed out.

Denise gave me a funny look. "No, but she loves animals, she'd probably enjoy coming along."

And I'd probably enjoy leaving her home, I thought to myself but didn't say. What I *did* say was, "Good idea. I'll ask her."

Surprise, surprise, Anna was thrilled. In fact, she was so happy about it I decided it wasn't that much of a bother letting her tag along. She skipped and sang happy nonsense songs all the way there, and talked Gabby into joining her in the kitten room while we put Denise's donations on the shelves.

"This is a lot of food and stuff," I said. "Where'd you get it all?"

"Neighbors, mostly. And my parents pick up a few things most weeks."

"Anna used to make regular contributions," I told her. "But she got *her* supplies from her blackmailing career."

Denise laughed. "Yeah, I know," she said. "She told me about it the first time she volunteered here. What a cutie pie."

"Easy to say when you're not on the paying end of her extortion schemes," I said. I tried to scowl, but a grin snuck through.

"So *enterprising*," Denise said. "So — are we going to talk about Steve?"

That caught me off guard, which I'm almost sure was her plan. "What about him?" I asked.

That earned me a raised eyebrow.

"Come on — you haven't said a word since the other night. Did he admit it? Are you guys okay?"

"Not really," I said. And then I told her everything.

She listened. She never interrupted once.

"Are you still sure it was him?" she asked gently.

"Pretty much, but you know what, I don't even care *who* it was anymore," I said.

"Then you'd better talk to Steve."

I didn't know if he'd let me in or not. The days of silence might have made things worse, so when I knocked at his door later, I had no idea what kind of reception I might be in for.

He looked surprised to find me standing there, and I braced myself for another door slam. It didn't happen.

"Hey," he said.

"I, uh, wanted to, uh, say I was sorry," I said.

"Go ahead then," he said.

"Well, I am. Sorry, I mean."

"Okay," he said.

And just like that, we were good. It wasn't much of a conversation, I know. Definitely not what Denise had in mind when she urged me to go talk to him. But that's how things are with some friends. I knew we'd sort out the details later, if we needed to. And we did, a couple of days later, hanging at my place.

It was Steve who brought it up.

"How'd you figure out it was Riley after all?" he asked, popping open a root beer.

I must have looked startled, because he understood instantly that I still thought it was him.

"Wait. You apologized and you still thought I did it?" he said.

"I don't care *who* it was," I said. "Everybody makes mistakes. It's not important."

He thought about that for a moment, took a long drink of pop and let out an even longer burp.

"Not bad," I said.

He grinned, but quickly grew serious again.

"I didn't do it, Derek. I *wouldn't*."

And I believed him. Which was weird, since I'd also been so sure Riley was telling me the truth.

"Hey, I think I know how you can narrow it down," Steve said. "At least ten different people sent it to me, once it was out there."

"So?" I said.

Steve was scrolling down his list of messages, but he paused to explain his theory.

"If we look to see who was sending it around first, that should give us a hint about the original sender."

"Makes sense," I said. If the earliest messages came from people connected to Riley, that would point to her. Oddly, I almost didn't want to know anymore.

Steve looked up from his phone. "Check yours too."

"My phone practically exploded with messages that night," I said, remembering the blast of alerts I'd received.

"So just check the first few that came in," he said.

I swiped my phone on and started scrolling. "Sorry, pal," I said when I found what I was looking for. "The first message I got was from Dayton."

Dayton is a pretty good friend of ours, which pointed the finger of blame squarely at Steve. I doubted if Riley even knew Dayton.

I opened the thread and turned the phone to show Steve. It wasn't much of a message — the video followed by a rude comment with a couple of laughing emoticons.

Steve glanced over. His eyes narrowed and then his head jerked.

"Give me that!" he said, reaching for my phone.

Once he'd grabbed it out of my hand he stared in silence for a few seconds. I could see he was about to laugh, which was odd considering it incriminated him.

"Dude," he said, passing it back. "The video is on the *right*."

I glanced down. "So?" I said, but even as the word

came out of my mouth, I got it.

"Ladies and gentlemen, we've found our culprit!" Steve said.

And we had. It was *me*. Dayton's text was in answer to the video *I* had sent *him*!

"Man, you must have butt-dialed or messed up some other way," Steve said as I slowly absorbed the truth.

It took a few minutes before it fully sank in. By then, I felt like crud. I'd accused two innocent people of something I'd done myself.

"Look, Steve—"

Steve stopped me right there.

"Forget it," he said, grinning. "Everybody makes mistakes. It's not important."

And he was right. I know that because, in the strangest way possible, everything that's happened has taught me a few things about what matters. And what doesn't.

ACKNOWLEDGEMENTS

Back in 2001 I sent out samples of my very first young adult novel, and was thrilled when three Canadian publishers asked for the full manuscript. Even as a newcomer to this industry, I understood my book would be best served with an editor who had a genuine commitment to the story. I quickly realized that Barry Jowett was that editor, and happily, my first publication (and a good many others) found a home with him.

It was, therefore, a real pleasure to find our paths connecting once again with this story. There is a sense of comfort and confidence in working with someone who was there at the start, and whose guidance you know you can trust.

Thanks, Barry.

VALERIE SHERRARD was born in 1957 in Moose Jaw, Saskatchewan, and grew up in various parts of Canada. Her father was in the Air Force so the family moved often, and was sent to live in Lahr, West Germany in 1968. There, her sixth grade teacher, Alf Lower, encouraged her toward writing, although many years would pass before she began to pursue it seriously.

Valerie's debut YA novel was published in 2002. Since then, she has expanded her writing to include stories for children of all ages.

Valerie Sherrard's work has been recognized on national and international levels and has been translated into several languages. She has won or been shortlisted for numerous awards, including the Governor General's Award for Children's Literature, The Canadian Library Association Book of the Year for Children, the TD Children's Literature, the Geoffrey Bilson, the Ann Connor Brimer, and a wide range of readers' choice awards.

Valerie currently makes her home in New Brunswick with her husband, Brent, who is also an author.

We acknowledge the sacred land on which Cormorant Books operates. It has been a site of human activity for 15,000 years. This land is the territory of the Huron-Wendat and Petun First Nations, the Seneca, and most recently, the Mississaugas of the Credit River. The territory was the subject of the Dish With One Spoon Wampum Belt Covenant, an agreement between the Iroquois Confederacy and Confederacy of the Ojibway and allied nations to peaceably share and steward the resources around the Great Lakes. Today, the meeting place of Toronto is still home to many Indigenous people from across Turtle Island. We are grateful to have the opportunity to work in the community, on this territory.

We are also mindful of broken covenants and the need to strive to make right with all our relations.